EFUA TRAORÉ

CHILDREN
OF THE
QUICKSANDS

EFUA TRAORÉ

CHILDREN OF THE QUICKSANDS

Chicken House

2 Palmer Street, Frome,
Somerset BA11 1DS
www.chickenhousebooks.com

First published in Great Britain in 2021
Chicken House
2 Palmer Street
Frome, Somerset BA11 1DS
United Kingdom
www.chickenhousebooks.com

Chicken House/Scholastic Ireland, 89E Lagan Road, Dublin Industrial Estate,
Glasnevin, Dublin D11 HP5F, Republic of Ireland

Cover and interior design by Helen Crawford-White
Typeset by Dorchester Typesetting Group Ltd
Printed and bound in Great Britain by CPI Group (UK) Ltd, Croydon CR0 4YY

FSC
www.fsc.org
MIX
Paper from
responsible sources
FSC® C020471

1 3 5 7 9 10 8 6 4 2

British Library Cataloguing in Publication data available.

PB ISBN 978-1-913322-36-6
eISBN 978-1-913696-05-4

For my daughters
Shola, Enina and Leila.
And in memory of Ese.

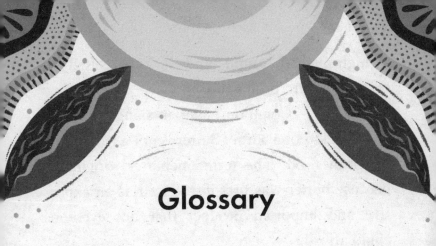

Glossary

AGBALUMO – A dark-orange forest tree fruit roughly the size of a mandarin. It has soft orange flesh with milky, sticky juice and large dark-brown kernels. The kernels are used to decorate ankle strings for dancing because they make a nice jingling sound. As kids we used to chew the skin until it turned to chewing gum.

AGBO – The leaves of a medicinal plant used to heal malaria and other illnesses. It is very bitter.

AGEGE BREAD – A famous soft, stretchy, sweet white bread that originated from a part of Lagos called Agege.

AGOGO – A very old musical instrument made of metal that is shaped like a cowbell and has a long handle. It is hit with a wooden stick to create a high-pitched sound and is often used in ceremonies in Yorubaland.

AJEBUTTER – Common Nigerian slang for a rich or spoilt kid or a softie. Butter is not a traditional Nigerian food. The term 'ajebutter' originated because butter was first introduced as an expensive and imported product that not everyone could afford.

AKARA – A fried spicy bean cake often eaten for breakfast with soft bread or corn porridge.

ASHE – Magical power.

AYO – A wooden board game with twelve pits into which round hazelnut-sized seeds are dropped. When I was little we sometimes played ayo in twelve small holes we had dug into the earth.

BATA DRUM – A double-sided drum of which one side is larger than the other. It is historically used by the Yoruba people in religious ceremonies.

BE-ENI – Yes.

CAFTAN – A tunic, traditionally worn in hot African and Middle Eastern climates. In Nigeria, caftans are formal wear, especially for men, and are often made with expensive materials and elaborately and stylishly embroidered.

CORAL BEADS – These are mined from coral stones in the oceans and are cut and polished as beads. They are important in Yoruba tradition as they are used to show royal status, wealth or age.

EFUN – A white chalk made of ground snail shell and white clay. It is used to draw magic symbols and to paint the body in traditional religious ceremonies to appease the gods and goddesses.

EGUN – Spirits of departed ancestors.

EWA AGOYIN – A meal of soft cooked beans eaten with a very spicy, peppery sauce made with palm oil and red bell peppers.

FILA – A soft hat traditionally worn by Yoruba men. It fits snugly on the head and can be worn tilted to one side, or with flaps on both sides, depending on the style.

GALAGOS – Also called a bushbaby. A nocturnal animal that looks like a little monkey with very large eyes. It has a lot of mysterious stories around it due to the fact that it cries like a baby. It is said to lure people into the forest at night with its cries.

GBEDU DRUM – The largest of the Yoruba drums. It signifies royalty and was traditionally only ever played in the presence of kings. It is played using an open palm and a stick. An old proverb says 'No thief will ever dare steal a gbedu drum'.

GELE – Large and elaborately styled headties made of firm and often shiny or colourful fabrics. They can be worn daily but are mostly worn to weddings, church or special events.

IJOKO – A wooden stool that may be carved with very intricate designs.

IRUKERE – A staff of office for a chief, made of horsetail hairs attached to a wooden handle. It is also used by priests and priestesses in religious ceremonies or held by traditional dancers.

JUJU – African magic and spiritual beliefs.

KOLANUT – The nut of a tree found in the African rainforests. The first taste is bitter, but then it sweetens after a while. It can be used like coffee to keep awake but can also be used as a medicine. It is often used ceremonially for guests or chiefs.

KOSI IBERU – No fear.

OFADA RICE – A type of unpolished rice famously eaten with ofada stew, which is made with locust beans.

OKADA – A slang term in Nigeria used for motorcycle taxis.

ORISHA – Deities, or gods and goddesses in Yoruba religion. The deities have different roles and powers.

SHEKERE – Shakers made from the gourds of a calabash tree and decorated with beads that rattle against the gourd to make music.

SHOKOTO – A traditional trouser in Yorubaland with a drawstring to fasten on the waist.

SUYA – Grilled meat skewers served with a red peppery spice and raw onions. It is a famous street food in Nigeria and is also commonly sold at the beaches in Lagos.

TALKING DRUM – An hourglass-shaped drum that is clamped under the arm and hit with a curved stick. By striking and holding the drum in a certain way, the drummer can mimic human speech and tones and can communicate messages.

ZOBO – A refreshing drink commonly served cold in Nigeria. It is made of dried hibiscus petals and other ingredients like orange, lemon or pineapple juice, ginger and honey.

1

Holidays at the
Other End of the World

Simi climbed into the taxi reluctantly. The seats were threadbare and it smelt as if the last passengers had been goats. She wrinkled her nose, desperately trying to suppress a new wave of anger and tears.

Her mum, who had just given the driver instructions, came around the car and put a slim hand on the still open door. Simi ignored her, folding her arms across her chest and looking straight ahead.

'Simi, it's only for two months,' her mum said softly.

She didn't reply.

'Please don't make this more difficult for me

than it already is. I am so happy to have found this new job. But I have to go to London for training and I can't leave you alone in Lagos for so long. And you know we really need the money now that your dad and I . . .' Her mum broke off.

Simi winced at the reminder of the divorce they had all gone through in the past year.

'Simi, believe me, if I had any other option, I would definitely have chosen it rather than send you there. But we do not have the money for any summer camps and I do not have any other family than *her*.' The way her mum always said 'her' made Simi really nervous about meeting her grandmother.

She felt her mum's eyes on her, hoping she would smile and say that she understood, that she forgave her. Simi did not look up. She had spent the last weeks begging. Telling her mum that she was thirteen and old enough to stay at home alone. That she could borrow the money for a summer camp from her dad, who definitely had enough of it. But her mum had shaken her head and ignored her pleas. So now she ignored her back.

Her mum sighed, then pulled something out of her handbag. It was a little envelope.

'This is for *her*,' she said. 'You must give it to her immediately. On the spot! And I mean as soon as you get there!'

Simi looked up, irritated. What was in the letter? And why was her mum acting so strangely again? All this secrecy really annoyed her. She didn't know anything about this woman who was supposed to be her grandmother. She hadn't even known that she existed until recently, when the holiday decision had been made. Just like that: '*You're going to your grandmother! That's where you will spend the school holidays!*'

And as far as Simi had understood, this grandmother lived in the middle of some jungle! A place called Ajao. She would even have gone to stay with her dad and his fancy new girlfriend instead. But her mum was too proud. She would never ask him or anybody else for help.

'Are you listening to me at all?' she asked impatiently. She held the letter under Simi's nose. 'It is very important that you give her the letter at once!'

'Yes, yes. OK,' Simi muttered and took it from her. She slid the envelope into her rucksack, which was on her lap. For a brief moment she felt her mum's hand on her shoulder. Then the rusty car door slammed shut with a rattle and Simi immediately felt the sticky air enclose her like a heavy blanket.

Simi suddenly panicked and rolled down the stuttering window to make one last attempt.

'Please, Mum! Can't you at least take me there? Only until . . .'

Her mum immediately took a step back. Her expression tolerated no further discussion and Simi gave up. She knew that stony, distant look all too well. Whenever it came to the subject of the past or her family, her mum fell silent and became a total stranger to her. The past was an absolute taboo. Simi had always assumed that her grandparents had died in a bad accident or something, and that her mum couldn't bear to talk about them.

She sighed. Now she would have to go alone to this grandmother that she had never met. And she would just turn up at her door unannounced. Her mum had come most of the way, taking the five-hour bus journey from Lagos with her. But now Simi was to travel the last stretch to Ajao in the taxi on her own.

'But what if she's not there?' she'd asked desperately on the bus earlier.

'She never goes anywhere,' her mum had replied dryly. 'Except into the forest to her heathen . . .' She had stalled before continuing more gently, 'She visits a few neighbours, but everyone knows where to find her.'

'Yes, but what if she is not, erm . . . not living there any more?' Simi had stammered. She had actually wanted to say 'alive'.

'She still lives in Ajao,' her mum had replied. 'And she is *alive*.'

'And what if she doesn't feel like having her granddaughter for two months without being asked?'

But her mum had just shaken her head. 'She'll take you in. She'll be very glad to see you.' And that had been the end of the matter.

Now her mum gave the old driver a few more instructions. His name was Mr Balogun, and he had been very excited to hear where he was to take her. He even recognized her mum from years ago.

'You will be in good hands with him,' her mum said as the car rattled to life.

And that was that.

2

Journey to the Unknown

The journey to Ajao turned out to be terribly exhausting. The untarred road was deeply rutted by rain and erosion, so that the driver only made slow and difficult progress. The car screeched and moaned so much that Simi worried they might not arrive in one piece.

To the left and right, the dense forest crowded into the road. Tall trees and bushes, higher and thicker than she had ever seen anywhere around Lagos, gave the road a pleasantly cool shade. But at the same time, the forest, towering high above them, felt threatening.

'What are these trees?' she asked the old driver, who hadn't spoken a word since they left.

'Trees?' He turned his gaze from the road to look at her, and she immediately worried about him not seeing the next pothole.

'What are those trees called? The tall ones,' she asked a little louder.

He looked at her from underneath his wrinkled eyelids. Brown teeth stained with kolanut flashed as his mouth split into a crooked grin. 'Iroko! This is iroko tree. Tree of spirits,' he said in a cracked voice.

She nodded quickly and breathed a sigh of relief when he finally turned back to face the road. *Tree of spirits*. His words echoed in her mind like ghostly whispers, and she felt queasy as she stared at the long-limbed trees.

'Woman, where I dey take you, she be your grandmother,' he said after a short while.

That didn't sound like a question but she felt she had to say something, so she replied, 'Yes.'

'Your grandmother, she be very good woman. People know am well-well.'

Well, not known by me, Simi thought, and looked out of the window listlessly.

After an hour's drive, as Simi had feared, there

was a loud crash and the car got stuck in a pothole. The driver made a hissing sound and clicked his tongue loudly.

'You go help me,' he grumbled over his shoulder.

He got out of the car, bent down and disappeared from view. Simi opened the door and climbed out gingerly.

The old man knelt in front of the car on the rough ground, muttering.

'Kiakia!' he suddenly called. 'Quick!' He pointed to the back of the car with a crooked index finger. 'Push!'

Simi stumbled quickly to the rear. A sudden rustling sound in the bushes beside her made her look around nervously. The huge iroko trees on both sides of the road trembled in the breeze and seemed to arch over her like agitated giants. Goosebumps formed on her skin as she remembered the driver's words.

'Push!' the driver called again.

Simi's head jerked up. The rustling from the bushes came again and she tried to put away all thoughts of snakes and other animals that might be lurking in the forest. She began to push the car with all the energy she could muster.

The car hardly budged.

What if they did not get the car out? she thought as she looked around fearfully. In the last half hour they had not driven past a single village or town, or seen a single person.

Simi pushed again with all possible force, sweat breaking out in her armpits. The driver heaved against the car at the same time and this time the car clattered briefly.

'More!' he shouted. He twisted the steering wheel through the open driver's door and pushed the car at the same time. Simi pushed with enough strength to burst her veins. She wanted to get out of this place as quickly as possible.

After three attempts, it worked. The car jerked out of the pothole.

'Kiakia!' the driver called again.

Simi jumped into the car, dusted off her dirty hands and breathed out in relief. As the car began to move again, she pulled a book from her ruck-sack and used it as a fan. The old man's driving was more cautious now, and gradually she became tired. She leant her head against the seat, despite the risk of her braids smelling of goat, and closed her eyes.

When Simi woke up, the car was slowing down and they were driving into a village. She sat up and looked out of the open window. Everything was the colour of dark red clay – the houses, the compounds and the road. Even the rusty iron roofs seemed to want to blend in.

On either side of this one red road Simi counted ten houses, which were not much more than little huts. She saw goats, chickens and naked toddlers running around. Under a tall mango tree two elderly men faced each other on a bench, playing Ayo. And as Simi watched the round seeds drop into the pits of the wooden game board, she groaned. No TV, no internet or phone to chat with friends, just a board game with seeds. How was she ever going to survive eight weeks here?

She glanced at her phone. Zero signal! She sighed. What had she expected?

At the end of the village, just before the road disappeared into the forest, was a tiny house made of the same reddish-brown clay as all the others. Two faded wooden shutters framed a single window beside an open front door.

The driver parked the car in front of it. They had arrived.

'Ajao!' he announced.

Two hibiscus bushes adorned the yard in front of the house. The leaves and flowers were covered with red dust, so even the plant was the same colour as the whole village. A large pot stood waist high next to the front door, a small cup hanging on a cord from the handle.

Suddenly, a tiny woman appeared at the threshold and Simi drew in her breath sharply.

She had a colourful yellow scarf tied around her head and she wore a floor-length green caftan. Cowry-shell bracelets dangled at her wrists and ankles, and she was barefoot.

Her grandmother was not quite as old as she had imagined, but she knew immediately that it was her because she looked exactly like her mum. And like Simi. They all had the same little nose, serious, sharp eyes and defiant mouth. Three generations with one and the same face.

Once again, Simi felt sad and confused. Why

had her mum been so secretive about her family? She climbed out of the car.

The old woman's sharp eyes were fixed directly on her.

The driver had already taken Simi's suitcase out of the boot and was carrying it to the door.

'Mr Balogun, welcome,' her grandmother said. 'How are you?' she greeted him, then looked right back at Simi.

'Ekuirole – good afternoon,' the driver replied. 'My body is fine, thank you.'

'Congratulations. I heard you got your eighth great-grandchild,' her grandmother said.

'Yes, Iyanla.'

'The gods have blessed you well.'

'Yes, I am a blessed man, thank you, Iyanla.' He placed Simi's suitcase in front of the door.

'Good evening, erm . . . grandmother,' Simi said bending her knees respectfully.

'Welcome, my child,' the old woman said. 'It is good that you have finally come.'

Simi did not know what to say. Her grand-mother did not appear in any way surprised to see her. She did not ask any questions. She just stood there in the doorway as if she had known that today she would get a visit from her granddaughter.

How many times had Simi tried to imagine this moment? Her fantasies of stuttered explanations, confusion, hugs or maybe even tears now seemed totally silly. She had a sudden feeling that you did not have to say much to this woman. Somehow, she already knew everything.

Simi had the very uncomfortable feeling her grandmother could read her mind.

The car coughed itself back into life.

'Duro. Wait,' her grandmother called. 'I have something for your grandchild!' She went inside.

Simi did not know if she should follow her or remain on the doorstep. She decided to wait.

The driver killed the engine and got back out of the car.

Her grandmother returned with a small package wrapped in banana leaves. The driver took it respectfully in both hands and bowed his head.

'Your granddaughter should rub the ointment on the baby after bathing her in the evening. It will keep illness away.'

'Ese gan,' he said, bowing again. 'Thank you, Iyanla'.

Her grandmother nodded. And when the driver was gone, she turned and went inside the house.

'Bags do not grow legs to carry themselves in this part of the country,' she called over her shoulder.

Simi took off her sandals, grabbed her suitcase and hurried in after her grandmother.

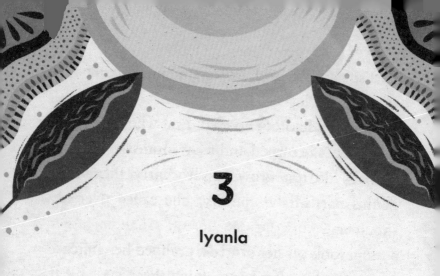

3

Iyanla

It was quite dark but pleasantly cool inside the little house. The floor under Simi's bare feet felt soothing and she was surprised to find that it was made of clean, polished red clay. Her eyes slowly adjusted to the dim light and she looked around. Her grandmother was nowhere in sight. There were two more doors, one closed and one open, leading into a tiny corridor.

In one corner of the room was a small table and a bed-like sofa covered with a hand-woven blanket in dark red and orange. Pretty yellow curtains covered the small window. A straw mat lay under the table, and on it stood a clay bowl with kolanuts. The decoration was simple but friendly.

Her mum preferred darker colours and mono-tones. Their little flat in Lagos was filled with all possible shades of grey.

Simi put down her heavy suitcase and her sandals, and walked gingerly through the open door towards the back of the house.

A tight corridor led into a slightly larger passageway, which obviously served as a store-room. On one side, Simi saw tall shelves filled with foodstuffs. Underneath, yams, green plan-tains, a large tin of palm oil and a bag of rice were neatly stored against the wall. On the other side, hundreds of little clay pots, vials and packages, wrapped in brown paper or dried leaves, lined the shelves. Simi stood and stared.

'Why do I have the feeling that you were sent here in ignorance?'

Simi jumped. She had not heard her grand-mother approach.

'In ignorance?' she asked, swallowing nervously.

'Your confusion is clearly carved into your face. And since I know your mother well, my name probably never crossed her lips.'

Simi shifted uncomfortably from one foot to

the other.

'She had no choice? Things were tight and she saw no other way out? Is she in trouble?' Her grandmother's eyes were so sharp now that Simi had to look away.

'How . . . how do you know? Did Mum call you after all?'

Her grandmother waved a hand. 'Do you see a telephone anywhere?'

Simi felt her face heat up and once again regretted her quick tongue, which was always a bit faster than her brain.

'You mean she did not even tell you what sleepy village she was sending you to? Were you expecting to find a telephone here?'

'No! I mean, yes, of course she told me, I, erm, I just forgot that.'

'May I now know what made your mother send her daughter to me when we have not spoken in years?'

'My parents got divorced . . . last year, and my mum has to travel for work,' Simi said slowly.

Even now, a year later, she did not like to talk about the divorce. She pushed the words out of her mouth and tried to ignore the bitter taste they left behind. Her dad's words to her mum in one of their many quarrels came back to her: *Nothing ever makes you happy . . . You carry anger around with you like a shield . . . You don't let any other feelings through . . . If you don't face up to your past, you will never be happy in life . . .* Was this her mum's way of trying to get back in touch with her past? Did she want to fix the broken relationship with her mother by sending her here? But if that was the case, why had she sent her here alone? And why could she still not bring herself to talk about the past?

Her grandmother made a face that was difficult to interpret.

'Is it OK, that I, erm . . . that I came here?'

Her grandmother walked to the shelves with the little pots and reached up to bring one down. She ignored Simi's question.

'What kind of job is it that separates a mother from her child?'

'She's a pharmacist. She just got a new job in an international company and she has to go to London for the training.'

Her grandmother's forehead creased and she looked confused.

'A pharmacist is someone who—' Simi began to explain.

'I know what a pharmacist is,' her grandmother interrupted irritably. 'Even though I live out here, I am not from yesterday.'

'I'm sorry,' Simi said, feeling very embarrassed.

'It is just that I am surprised that your mother chose this work. I would not have thought . . .'

Her grandmother stopped and shook her head. Simi was not sure, but was it a brief flash of pride that she saw in her grandmother's face? She was obviously a kind of herbalist, a traditional pharmacist, so to speak.

Her grandmother took out a small cloth bag from a larger container.

'Come, we have a lot to do today,' was all she said, and slipped out to the backyard.

The first part of the yard was covered, and underneath the roof was a large wooden table with two chairs on one side. Next to it was a traditional open firewood-hearth with a three-legged pot balanced on soot-blackened stones. A fire blazed under the pot.

The rest of the yard was swept clean and surrounded by a low wooden fence. At one end stood a large frangipani tree that stretched its long arms across the backyard and provided shade.

Beside the tree was a small round well, and next to this a herb garden. Butterflies and bees flew about, and Simi could smell fresh thyme. Her mum loved thyme and even grew it in their tiny Lagos garden. Simi tried to imagine her mum as a little girl here, bent over the thyme and breathing in its scent. But she couldn't. She had never even seen a single picture of her mum as a child. Simi sighed and stared beyond the fence. A path ran into a thick forest one way, and the other way back towards the village.

Her grandmother had already seated herself at the table.

'Are you hungry?' she asked.

Simi thought for a moment – her stomach still felt queasy from the bumpy journey. She shook her head. 'Can I use the bathroom?'

Iyanla tossed her head in the direction of a tiny

shed made of rusty metal sheets at the far corner of the courtyard. Simi opened one of two metal doors that were almost hidden behind elephant grass. The door squeaked noisily and she stared into an empty space. The floor was laid out with many small stones and there was a clothes line stretched across on which a towel hung.

This was the shower!

Well, what had she expected? Where there was no electricity, there was often no running water.

She opened the other door, already dreading what she would find. In a corner was a bucket of water and in front of her a square, wooden construction, like a wooden box. On top of it was a round, plate-sized wooden cover. This was the toilet! *Wow, how did I end up here?* she thought, trying not to think of her nice little bathroom at home with its shiny white tiles and soft grey rug.

When she came back out, her grandmother pointed for her to sit. She was leaning over a large bowl on the floor next to the table. From the brightly coloured towels and kitchen utensils she pulled out a small stone pestle and a mortar. She put them on the table in front of Simi. Then she placed some dried leaves in the mortar from the little pot she had taken from inside the house. She added black powder from a tiny clay bowl. Then she got a small bottle containing a thick yellow liquid that looked like peanut oil and added a few drops.

'Grind,' she said, pushing the stone pestle towards Simi.

At first uncertain, Simi began to stir carefully with the pestle, then, getting bolder, she began to grind the leaves with more force. Back home, she loved helping her mum in the kitchen. Her mum was uncomplicated when cooking. The deep worry lines between her eyebrows were smoothed away when she was preparing ewedu soup or chopping vegetables for fried rice, and Simi always enjoyed these relaxed moments with her.

While Simi worked, her grandmother plucked a sprig from a tall bush in the garden. She removed the dark green leaves – they looked like bitter-leaf, which her mum often used to make soup – and washed them in a bowl. Then she sat down at the table with a small knife and a board.

'What does she call you?' she asked suddenly.

'Sorry?' Simi replied, confused.

'What did your parents name you? Surely you have a name?' Her grandmother looked at her with a raised eyebrow.

'Simi,' she replied. And after a moment's hesitation, she said her full name. 'Oluwanifesimi.'

Her grandmother nodded in satisfaction. 'That is a good name to own. You know what it means?'

'Yes. *God loves me.*'

Her grandmother nodded again. 'It is good when the gods are on your side.'

Simi looked up, surprised at the use of the plural form of 'gods'. It was the second time since she arrived. But Iyanla's face remained unreadable, though the hardness of her face had loosened. Simi could see signs of white hair under the yellow headscarf and her grandmother's posture was bent – she had narrow shoulders and a slightly rounded back, but she did not have a single wrinkle on her face. She wore such a peaceful expression as she chopped the herb that Simi felt bold enough to ask her the question that was at the front of her mind.

'Grandma? Why did you and mum quarrel?'

'Iyanla!' her grandmother interrupted her. 'Just call me Iyanla, "big mother". That is what everyone calls me. It means the same thing. If you call me "Grandma", I will feel as if I am back at the white man's school.' Iyanla paused briefly, then added, 'It was not really a quarrel.'

Simi nodded, even though her question had not been answered. Maybe it was too early for that conversation. She watched Iyanla chop the leaves, the cowry shells at her wrists dancing with each movement and her quick fingers keeping the leaves in place. Simi tried to picture her as a little girl in some missionary school some sixty or seventy years ago, but couldn't.

For a while they were quiet. But the silence was not unpleasant. It only felt surreal, like in a dream. Sitting at the edge of a huge forest in the middle of nowhere, stirring strange mixtures.

Suddenly, into the silence, came loud cries, and they were coming closer. Iyanla stopped what she was doing and raised her head.

'We have visitors,' she said with a sigh. 'Visitors with problems, it seems.' She got up and rinsed her hands in the basin. 'Why don't you take a little walk, my child?'

Simi nodded, but now she was feeling worried again.

'If you go out there, the path to the right leads towards the village.' Iyanla pointed to the little gate in the fence. 'Walk past the houses, then you will find a big ube tree at the other end of the village. The only one of its kind in Ajao. You can check for ripe ube and collect some. There is always a long stick beside the tree.' She handed her a small woven basket.

Simi nodded again, but wondered if she would find the tree. She loved eating the little dark purple fruits but she had never seen an ube tree before.

'Make sure you turn right, not left!' Iyanla repeated, with a frown. 'And do not be gone for too long. It will be dark in an hour and you do not want to be outside at nightfall.'

Iyanla gathered her long robe and looked irresolutely at the unfinished mixtures on the table. The voices were much louder now. They spoke very quickly in Yoruba, and it was difficult for Simi to understand.

'I hope that this will not take too long,' said Iyanla, heading for the house. 'When you come back, we will eat.'

As if on second thoughts, she stopped and turned. She put her hand to her throat and pulled out a chain from underneath her dress. A beautiful greenish-blue stone in a copper setting hung from it. Iyanla placed the necklace in Simi's hand.

'Here, my child. This is for you,' she said. 'It makes an old woman very glad that your mother sent you here.' She disappeared into the house.

'Thank you, Iyanla,' Simi called after her in surprise, but she was already gone.

4

The Forest of Ajao

Simi looked closely at the necklace. The stone was a transparent colour somewhere between blue and green, like a deep river on a sunny day. She noticed tiny bubbles in it too, making it look even more like a drop of water.

She fastened the chain carefully around her neck, feeling happy about such a special gift. Then she sneaked in quickly after Iyanla, hoping the visitors were not in the house, because she had to get her sandals. Through the window she saw a young boy who was being supported by a woman. His hand was covered in blood and his face was wet with tears. Simi squirmed at the sight and looked away. The woman holding him spoke gentle words to calm him while a chattering crowd of children surrounded them and another woman was talking to Iyanla. A baby wrapped in a colourful cloth around a girl's back was screaming.

Iyanla held up her hands and shouted, 'Quiet! Everybody quiet.'

Simi was startled by the calm that immediately came over the crowd. She backed away from the window, grabbed her sandals and walked quietly out of the back door.

She snatched the basket from the table outside and walked past the herb garden and through the little gate. She stood in the middle of the path and looked around. A tiny stream, almost overgrown with grass and other water plants, trickled alongside the path. To the right the path looked wider and more used. To the left, it was barely visible and, after a few metres, it disappeared into a thicket of ferns and bushes under towering trees.

Just as she was about to turn right towards the village, as Iyanla had instructed, Simi thought she heard a strange sound and stood still. She listened, cocking her head towards the forest. There it was again. A quiet, vibrating melody that rippled through the air, reminding her of winds swishing over the distant sands of Lekki Beach back home. It was gripping. Her nerves tingled strangely in her body. The next moment it was gone and she wondered if she had really heard it.

She realized that, without noticing, her feet had actually taken her towards the left and into the forest. The air here was cool and pleasant.

Suddenly, she heard laughter. A high-pitched, screaming laugh, clearly that of a monkey. How amazing! She felt like a *National Geographic* reporter, right at the source of nature, in the middle of the wilderness. Curiosity took over and she decided to peek further into the forest. She would take only very few steps. Her heart pounded at the thought of seeing some cute monkeys. Real, live monkeys in the wild. Then at least she would have something exciting to report at school after the holidays. Her friend Taye had flown to her cousins in America, and Chinwe had gone to Enugu, where her parents had their family home with a pool.

She was the only one who had to spend her

holidays in the wilderness. *It should at least be worth something*, she thought. She picked up a long stick she found at the side of the path. She definitely did not want to collide with snakes or any other wild animals without some form of protection. She was not going to be unprepared like some helpless and naïve city girl.

Just a few steps, she thought, and then she would go and pluck ube.

The forest was not even as dense as it looked at first glance. The narrow path snaked around huge tree trunks with thick, gnarled roots that dug into the ground. She could see pretty far through the bushes and treetops. But there were no monkeys swinging from branch to branch, no great gorges, dark caves or anything even half as exciting as that. The forest remained absolutely monotonous. She looked back, and could no longer see her grandmother's house. Only the greens of the forest all around her. She suddenly felt foolish standing in the middle of the jungle with a stick in her hand, and wondered what had made her do such a reckless thing.

She shook her head and was just about to hurry

back when she heard a creaking noise behind her. She turned and found herself staring into the yellow eyes of a grim-faced, ragged-looking man. He sat on a heavily laden rusty bicycle, plantains piled up in a big basket behind him. She jumped backwards on shaky legs into the scrub to let him pass.

'Ekuirole,' she greeted him when she found her voice again.

He did not reply. He just looked at her with his yellowing eyes and muttered something which sounded like 'the madness'. His voice sounded rough, as if he seldom used it. 'You should not be here,' he said. 'You must go home.' Then he shook his head before he continued riding his rusty bicycle along the uneven forest path.

A shiver ran down Simi's spine, but at the same time she felt the blood rise in her face. She was annoyed at his unfriendly behaviour. Maybe it was her pronunciation, she thought uneasily. She was aware that her Yoruba was not so good and that she spoke with an accent. Her father had often told her to be more diligent in learning it. He spoke to her in Yoruba, but, like her mother, she had always responded in English.

The thought of her parents, and in particular the thought of her parents before the divorce, suddenly made her sad. If they hadn't divorced, maybe they would have gone on a trip together somewhere nice, like two years ago, when they had travelled to Jos and strolled through the wildlife park and eaten strawberries grown in Nigeria on the high Jos plateau. Then she wouldn't be spending her holidays here all alone, in this remote village which felt like the end of the world. She noticed how the burst of energy that had made her so adventurous seeped out of her bones. She turned to walk back when she heard the strange melody again.

It began like the sound of a vibrant wind scattering sands. But then the swishing sound grew louder, gathering into a high, rippling tune. It was birdsong – so beautiful and so haunting that she stood motionless, her feet glued to the spot. The tune continued, persistent and urging, and Simi felt sure that it was calling her.

She turned, her feet moving in the direction of the song, and left the main trail, passing through bushes that scratched her legs. Somehow she could not stop walking. The forest around her began to change. It became denser. The air grew heavier and more humid with each step, the trees higher and the undergrowth thicker. Long vines hung down from the tall trees, almost touching the undergrowth.

Only ten more steps, then I'll turn back, she thought, but she kept going.

Only twenty more steps . . .

At some point, she couldn't tell how many steps she had taken.

She finally came to a standstill in the middle of a clearing and drew in a sharp breath.

In front of her lay a dreamy little red lake. In the middle of it was a grey rock, its smooth surface glowing in the fading light. A tall tree stood at the edge of the lake and leant over as if to protect the water below it. It was an iroko, she saw at once – the tree of spirits.

She looked up and saw a bird sitting in the branches of the iroko. She instinctively knew that it was this bird that had lured her here. Even though it was so high up, she saw its shiny gold plumage clearly through the leaves. How had it managed to bring her here? She felt as if she was standing beside herself. As if she had lost control over her own body. And now, she had the insistent feeling that something was about to happen. The air seemed to crackle.

As she watched the bird, it left the treetop, fluttered to the rock and sat upon it. The movement was quick and ghostly, like a reflection against the dark background of the forest. Its beady black eyes glittered as it stared at her. She understood immediately. The bird wanted her to come. And even though she wanted to run back to Iyanla's house as fast as possible, she could not control her feet.

She put one foot in front of the other and moved towards the lake.

5

Quicksands

The great rock in the middle of the lake now glowed red in the light of the setting sun, which seeped in through the treetops. The little bird was a golden spot on the rock.

Simi could not avert her eyes. Her heart pounded and there was a loud noise in her ears, as if a strong wind was blowing inside them. The reddish water seemed alive: it was thick and churned with snake-like waves. Even though all her senses were screaming out to her to turn around, she still moved forward. It was as if an invisible rope had been tied around her hips and was pulling her. She sensed that something was terribly wrong and that it was very important to turn back. But she could not. When she reached the shore of the lake and felt the sand fill her sandals, it was already too late.

She felt herself sink ankle-deep and then knee-deep into thick, swirling red sand. A memory came to her – her mum's fear of water – but she could not do anything against the pull on her legs.

The little bird watched from the rock. A moment ago it had looked pretty and bright, now it turned into an ugly grey bundle of feathers and flew back up into the iroko tree, leaving a dusty trail in the air. Then it disappeared into thin air.

Instantly Simi could think clearly again. She began to struggle to get back to firmer ground, but it was useless. She screamed when she realized she was stuck. Not only that, she was sinking deeper and deeper into the sand with every movement she made. Quicksand! It was like an invisible hand tugging at her feet.

'Help,' she screamed. 'Help me!' Her voice was so loud it broke.

But the only reply she heard was a loud flutter around her as frightened birds scattered out of the forest. Her cries for help were lost in the crown of the tall iroko tree that watched impassively as the sand swallowed her up.

The sand felt cold and wet, and it made disgusting, smacking sounds as she struggled. Suddenly, it gave way entirely and she was sucked in, whirling wildly through thick, sandy liquid. Sideways, forward, over, in all directions. She tried to fight against the swirl, but it was useless. The sand didn't let go of her and she had no idea where up or down was anyway. Her lungs were almost bursting and, just when she thought it was over and she was going to die, the quicksands spat her out.

She hit hard ground, a sharp pain driving through her head and shoulders. Coughing and gasping for air, it took her a long moment to calm down.

At last, still panting, she looked up. She was not in the jungle of Ajao any more.

This was a different place.

She turned in panic, trying to recognize something. What had happened? Where was she?

She was in a valley. In front of her, red sandhills

lined both sides of a wide path. They were of a strange, uneven texture, with cracks and dark crevices, as if hundreds of huge anthills had been pushed together. The path between them curved away from her, disappearing into redness. At the top of the hills were trees with weird brown leaves and black, yellow-mottled nuts. Even the dark sky looked wrong, almost purple. It was all wrong.

Where was the forest? The rock? Where was the lake?

A squishing sound made her turn abruptly, and she yelped in fear. A small red lake quivered in front of her, a mass of churning sand waves, slow and heavy, that every now and then made slurping noises. More sandhills enclosed the lake, forming a dead end. The only path was the one that led away from the lake and through the valley.

Simi took two steps back, away from the red heaving mass, and realized she had lost her sandals. The ground beneath her bare feet was soft and gave way as if she was walking on a mattress. Her footprints filled with watery red sand then smoothed out immediately.

A terrible thought shot through her mind. She

began to heave and gasp for air.

Was she dead?

Please, don't let me be dead, she prayed softly.

She took a large gulp of air and shook her head.

No. She couldn't be dead. She would have felt it, that moment of dying. She pinched her arm and felt the pain clearly. After death, she was sure no one felt pain.

But something was not right here. What place was this? What had happened to her? The hills around her, she noticed, were trembling and swaying. The whole valley seemed to be in a gentle kind of motion. As if everything was made of quicksand.

Simi felt dizzy and began to shiver. Her dress was dripping wet.

It was then that she heard whispering, echoing sounds, like distant voices from beyond the sandhills, and they seemed to be coming closer.

She turned in panic. Where could she hide? Spotting a crevice in one of the sandhills, she ran to it and, pushing aside the grass in front of it, slipped through the crack. Inside was a tiny hollow. She huddled there, panting and shaking all over. She clenched her hands tightly in her lap, trying to calm down.

Simi felt cold and alone and suddenly thought of her parents. A desperate sob escaped her throat and she put a hand over her mouth. She almost choked as a wave of despair swept through her insides. Tears trickled down her cheeks.

She forced herself to concentrate. She had to leave this place. She had to find a way back.

The voices sounded quite close now.

Her first impulse was to call for help and run out, but she stayed in her hiding place. She would see who it was first.

Two children arrived at the lake. They were boys of maybe ten years old. They each wore a rough brown cloth that was knotted over one shoulder and reached down to their knees. They were barefoot and carried long spears.

'There is no one here,' one said.

'No. Nothing,' the other replied.

They went back and forth, searching. Simi did not dare to move and hoped they would not look in her direction. Fortunately, she was well hidden.

'It was a false alarm,' the taller one said. 'A leaf lost in the quicksands?'

'But Layo felt it,' said the smaller one.

'Yes, but there is obviously no one here!'

Simi understood the children from her position relatively well, even though they were speaking Yoruba in a really strange way. Every sentence ended in a high-pitched tone like a question, even if it was not one.

'Well, then, come on. Let's go back and tell Layo before he gets angry that it is taking too long.'

'But he'll be very angry that we have no new-one for him,' said the little one, sounding anxious.

'It is not our fault that there is no new-one here and that he was wrong. Come.'

Simi watched them run away and took a deep breath of relief, leaning weakly against the sand wall in her little cave. Suddenly the solidity in her back gave way and wobbled, and it felt as if the wall was sucking her in.

She yelped and pulled herself out of its grasp. She tumbled out of the cave, sweat breaking out on her body as she crouched behind the grass. Fearfully, she looked around. The boys were gone.

She had to leave this place at once.

She walked cautiously to the convulsing red

lake and looked around desperately. She had to find the spot where the ghostly bird had lured her through the forest to the quicksands. But nothing seemed familiar. No forest, no rock. Only the lake was the same.

Her heart pounded painfully in her chest. She dreaded the thought that had just come to her, but she knew exactly what she had to do to find her way back. She moved closer to the lake and her heart raced even faster. Very slowly and very carefully she dipped her big toe into the red water. It swallowed her toe instantly. The watery mud began making greedy, sucking sounds and began tugging at her foot. She pulled her toe out, gasping.

Loud excited calls began to echo between the rows of trembling red hills, this time sounding like howls. She turned and saw a crowd of children running. Their spears were raised and aimed in her direction. Leading them was a tall, muscular boy. They were running towards her, shouting. She did not understand the words, but she knew they were not coming as friends. She was in danger.

Without any further thought, Simi took a deep breath and jumped into the quicksands.

6

A Delayed Letter

Again, she was whirled around terribly. Again, she thought her lungs would burst. And again, at the moment when she thought she would die, the thick sand spat her out.

She cried out as her already sore head hit hard ground, then she lay still for a moment, feeling dizzy and confused. When she opened her eyes, she nearly cried to find herself back under the iroko tree in the forest behind Iyanla's house.

It was almost completely dark now and the thought of running through the forest in the darkness made her tremble.

But she scrambled up and ran as fast as she could. She gasped as she trod on something sharp, but she did not stop running. The bushes on either side of the tiny path scratched mercilessly at her legs – she ignored them. When she finally saw the end of the forest, she was hobbling. A gust of hot wind ripped through the trees and the air felt electrified. From one moment to the next it began to rain heavily. The rain beat down like angry needles. Terrified, she tried to run faster but a few seconds later the wind roared through the trees again and the rain was gone. Simi stared at the dark sky, shivering. What was going on here?

A figure appeared in the middle of the path in front of her and Simi screamed.

It was Iyanla. She was holding up a kerosene lantern, her shadow long and dark.

'Do they not teach the children of big-big cities the difference between left and right?' she said.

Simi couldn't speak. She just stood there, panting, her eyes wide.

'Where are the ube?'

Simi gasped when she realized she must have lost the basket in the quicksands, along with her sandals.

'I lost the basket. I . . .' she began, but felt

confused. What had happened to her? Simi touched the back of her hurting head and grimaced. 'I am sorry,' was all she could think to say.

Iyanla turned and began to walk back towards her house. 'The forest is forbidden!' Her voice was sharp and Simi could hear the anger in it. 'I cannot believe I need to explain that forests are dangerous, especially at night.'

Simi lunged forward to stay close to her grand-mother and the light of the lantern. She felt absolutely ashamed and stupid.

'Where are your shoes?' Iyanla asked without looking back.

'I lost them as well,' Simi replied. But when she realized how pathetic that sounded, she quickly added, 'There was . . . a sound like a wild animal, and I ran so fast that I lost them.'

What she had just experienced seemed so un-believable and so surreal that she pushed it away to the very back of her mind. She must have hit her head really hard to have imagined such strange things. She hurried after Iyanla with trembling legs.

*

At Iyanla's house, Simi slowly came back to herself. She washed her feet and changed her wet clothes and Iyanla gave her a pair of flip-flops. Now she sat exhausted on the three-legged ijoko in the courtyard behind the house, warming herself by the fire. She forced herself not to think about what had happened and focused instead on everything her grandmother did.

Iyanla was stirring a large pot over the fire. She had not spoken a word since they got back. She had pointed to the stool and given Simi a blanket to drape over her shoulders. Now she handed her a cup with some of the liquid from the pot. The cup was a half calabash, cut out of the dried gourd of a calabash tree. In Lagos, Simi had only seen them used as decoration. She took it from Iyanla and in the dim light of the fire saw that it contained a dark green liquid.

'Drink,' Iyanla said.

Simi sipped the drink carefully. It was bitter, like black tea that had steeped too long, but after a few minutes she felt soothing warmth spread through her chest and crawl into her stomach. She soon began to feel better.

Iyanla placed her hands on her waist and looked up at the dark sky, her eyebrows drawn together. 'The rains are refusing to come,' she said. 'Those few drops were not even enough to remove dust from dry leaves. I wonder what the goddesses are up to. It is as if Oya and Oshun are angry. The air, the waters, the winds . . . they are all bristling with quiet rage.'

Simi wasn't sure what to make of her grandmother. She was like someone out of a storybook, talking about goddesses being angry and winds bristling with rage. But then she remembered the winds and the sharp rain in the forest and shivered. That *had* felt weird. She stared at the sky, which seemed quite normal, and the memory of the strange sky in that strange place came back. The whole experience seemed so unreal to her. She pushed the thoughts of quivering sandhills and terrifying quicksands out of her head. It was like a bad dream. She must have fallen unconscious in that lake and dreamt all those things. She shivered at what could have happened to her.

She shook her head and concentrated on the sounds around her. The night was empty of human-made sounds yet heavy with noise. In Lagos, at night you heard cars, horns, music from loudspeakers, calls from the mosques, singing and praying from the churches, hawkers quarrelling on the streets. Here, there was a regular chirping that had to be crickets singing in rhythm with a group of croaking frogs in the stream behind the house. Something buzzed nearby. A night owl called dully across the night sky, and some other animal whose grunts she did not recognize joined in. And in the distance she heard the monkeys again. Beside her ear a mosquito was singing in high soprano. It was like an amazing bush orchestra.

Iyanla lit another kerosene lamp and put it on the table. She had prepared a delicious meal. As if she had known that fried plantains with brown beans was Simi's favourite food. Simi's mouth watered at the sight and she plunged into it.

After a few minutes, she looked up and noticed that Iyanla was watching her very seriously. She paused, then quickly swallowed her mouthful.

'I'm sorry, Iyanla. I was so hungry that I did not wait for you. Are you not eating anything?'

Iyanla's serious face relaxed and Simi got a small idea of what she would look like when she smiled.

'No, I do not eat so late, my child, do not worry about me.'

'It tastes very good,' Simi said as she attacked the food again.

Iyanla fetched a bowl and set it down on the table. Simi watched her take out black pods and split them open. Small black beans that looked like pearls in the light of the lamp popped out. Iyanla focused on the pods, saying nothing. The crackling of the pods and the scratching of Simi's fork against the plate mingled with the sounds of the night.

When Simi finished eating, she picked up her plate and got up.

'Ese – thank you,' she said to Iyanla, and washed her plate in the bowl of water in which Iyanla had washed a spoon earlier. Then, wanting to be helpful, she grabbed a broom made of palm fronds to sweep together the pods that had fallen off the table.

'You are not really planning to sweep, are you?' Iyanla said, gripping her arm.

'Erm, I am not?' Simi stuttered.

'You want to sweep all your riches and blessings away?'

Simi looked at her blankly.

'Did no one ever tell you that one does not sweep at night?'

Simi shook her head and dropped the broom quickly without a word.

The owl hooted again, sounding much closer. Iyanla stared at the forest. 'If that owl hoots a third time behind my house then I will need ashe,' she muttered.

Simi dared not ask what ashe was. She had a feeling it would be some scary magic spell.

Iyanla turned back towards her, index finger raised in warning. She lowered her voice to a croaky whisper. 'No sweeping at night and no whistling at night either. The night has ears and it is in the cover of darkness that evil spirits begin to go about their business.'

Iyanla walked to the little back gate and closed it firmly. Her body was tense and she began to hum. Then she raised her right hand and circled it over her head three times, muttering, 'Kosi iberu in this house'. Simi knew that in Yoruba 'kosi iberu' meant 'no fear'.

Iyanla came and placed a little vial on the table. 'Against the mosquitoes. Rub it on your body.'

Gratefully, Simi dripped some of the liquid into her palm and rubbed it on herself. She already had some burning mosquito bites on her arms. The oil smelt fresh and spicy.

'This one is for the wounds on your legs and feet.' Iyanla passed her a cup containing a thick brownish paste.

Simi applied the paste, which smelt less appealing, to her feet before she slipped them back into her flip-flops.

In the meantime, Iyanla had set up a kind of incense burner on the table. She lit a candle beneath the rusty-looking burner and threw in some grass-like herbs. 'We must keep the air free of evil,' she said as she saw Simi's questioning look. Then she added some drops of oil and a little chunk of something that looked like black soap.

'The forest is forbidden.' Iyanla's voice was quiet as she repeated the warning. 'Do you understand me?'

Simi nodded quickly.

'This is Ajao. This is not Lagos. This place has juju. It has good but it also has evil. There are Egun, the evil spirits, and other creatures of the night out there. In Ajao we are one with the earth and with nature, which is the source of all power. You cannot do whatever you feel like here without thinking. Something could have happened to you in that forest. Your mother would not have forgiven me.'

Simi looked at Iyanla gloomily. She wanted to tell her that nothing would ever make her go back to the forest. She had probably experienced some sort of magical juju experience – a kind of trance after falling and hitting her head. She was lucky to have come back alive and in one piece.

Iyanla suddenly looked tired. 'I see that we have to teach you a lot of things. I am surprised your mother did not at least warn you about the forest. Did she not mention it?'

Simi shook his head.

'That is strange,' Iyanla continued. 'And you were not supposed to tell me anything? No message at all?'

'Oh, but yes!' Simi exclaimed, jumping up, startled. 'Sorry, I totally forgot.'

She ran into the house and fetched her rucksack with a very guilty conscience. Her mother had said at least five times that she should give the letter to Iyanla immediately upon her arrival. The letter was slightly rumpled and she smoothed it before handing it to Iyanla.

Iyanla made no move to take it from her. 'Read it to me,' she said. 'The written words of the white man are always so ridiculously small. I would rather search for dust between grains of rice than read his letters.'

Simi opened the letter and held it up to the kerosene lamp. It looked quite short. Her mum obviously had very little to say, even though she had not had contact with Iyanla for years.

She read out loud:

Iyanla,
I am sending you your granddaughter.
I am in a difficult situation and I have no other option. But maybe it is also time that Simi gets to know her grandmother.

Please do not tell her any of your superstitious stories. She has been raised as a Christian and should learn nothing about your gods and myths. Where that can lead is something we have unfortunately already seen with devastating consequences.

Most important of all: it is forbidden for her to go to that place or even into the forest. I know at least on this point we will agree.

I ask you to respect my wishes.

Biola

P.S. I arranged with Mr Balogun that he should pick her up in two months, on the last day of the school holidays.

Simi was shocked and ashamed. How could her mum be so distant and cold to her own mother? What could have happened between them?

The whole time she was reading, Iyanla stared into the fire with no sign of emotion. Simi looked at the letter again. Why did she have the terrible feeling that on the very day of her arrival she had gone exactly where her mum had clearly forbidden?

'What is this forbidden place?' she asked Iyanla softly.

Her grandmother looked up at her with sharp eyes. 'You read the letter yourself. Your mother does not want me to talk to you about any gods or "myths". She knows there are things that exist, things that have happened, but she refuses to speak about them, refuses to believe in them.'

Iyanla, who had seemed so calm up till now, was visibly upset. She got up, grabbed a chunk of firewood and threw it on the fire.

'Your mother wants to live in a world padded with cotton and soft cloths,' she continued. 'So that everything is very gentle and you can never hurt yourself. But there is no such thing. Real life is rough and spiky like the stem of a palm tree. And whether you like it or not, once in a while, when journeying through life and plucking its fruit, you will get scarred by it.'

There was an odd silence.

Simi knew exactly what Iyanla meant. Her mum always preferred to avoid uncomfortable discussions and immediately retreated into her shell. Now Simi was beginning to feel annoyed. If her mum had opened up, had clearly told her about this forbidden place, then she wouldn't have gone there and could have spared herself that terrible experience. All the secrecy was really annoying and now Iyanla was also refusing to explain things because of her mum.

'All my life, Mum has treated me like I was made of glass,' she said. 'She always wants to protect me, always seems afraid for me. I know it has something to do with the past. But she never talks about it.'

Iyanla nodded thoughtfully. 'I will tell you everything. You have a right to know. And I have already grieved your mother. I could not make it worse.' She paused. 'I think then it will also be easier for you to understand why she became the way she is.' She looked back into the fire. There was a pain in her eyes that she tried to hide by looking away, but Simi saw it.

'It is too late this night to swallow the thick lumps of such a heavy story.' Iyanla got up. 'The time is not yet ripe. Let us prepare the bed for you.'

Simi sighed, but at the idea of falling into bed

she realized how tired she was after her long day and terrible experience. She took one last look at the dark, looming shape of the forest, then joined Iyanla inside.

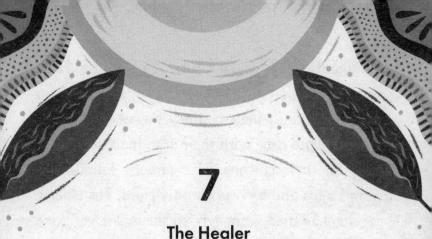

7

The Healer

It was pitch-black outside when Simi was awakened by soft movements in the house. She was still tired but when she remembered the events of the previous day she jumped up, wide awake. She rummaged in the dark living room for her toothbrush and toothpaste, and headed for the backyard.

Outside, the air was cool. The horizon was beginning to split the darkness with a thin, bright line. Birds twittered softly at the top of the frangipani tree and the air smelt of earth and fresh herbs. A cock crowed somewhere and Simi was suddenly filled with excitement. She was actually in a tiny village in the middle of the bush and it felt like she was part of a surreal adventure. How envious she had always been of her friends, who always drove to their country homes for Christmas to spend time with their grandparents and to meet all their cousins. Her father's family was from Lagos and he was an only child. His elderly parents had died years ago, so she had never gone to visit any extended family anywhere. Until now, she only knew city life. Now she too would finally get to know village life.

Unfortunately, the village of her grandmother was much more remote than the home towns of her friends, which at least had electricity and running water. And, yes, she had no cousins to hang out with, but somehow today she found it really cool to be in Ajao. And even though she still had a queasy feeling in her stomach about the day before, she was also excited about what more Iyanla might tell her.

She made her way across the yard and filled a cup of water from one of the buckets. Then she went between the bushes behind the herb garden and brushed her teeth in the greyness of dawn.

When she came back, Iyanla was seated at the table mixing some salves again. She was gnawing at a chewing stick that jutted out of the corner of her mouth.

'Good morning, Iyanla,' she called to her cheerfully.

'A good morning for you, too,' Iyanla answered. 'I see we slept well.'

An hour later, Simi trotted beside Iyanla carrying a basket of various salves and vials. The sun had only just shown itself and had not even begun to make its way up the sky, but Simi already knew that it would be a hot day. The air had become increasingly heavy and there was not even a breath of wind.

She had hoped to spend the day listening to Iyanla's stories, but quickly realized her grand-mother was too busy for that. She was obviously responsible for medicine and solving many other problems in the village.

At the hut of the first family they visited, a small boy lay ill on a mattress under a palm tree, his young mother sitting next to him. She immediately got up and greeted Iyanla respectfully, smiling warmly.

'Kikelomo, this is my granddaughter,' Iyanla said, squatting to look closely at the little boy.

Simi greeted Kikelomo, who smiled at her.

'How is he today?' Iyanla asked, her hand on the boy's forehead.

Kikelomo's face took on a worried look. 'The night was tough,' she said softly.

The boy was awake but made no move to get up. He looked very pale. Iyanla spoke soothing words to him as she brought out a flat vial and began to rub his chest with an ointment.

'Did he cough a lot again?'

'Yes, all night. I gave him a lot to drink, as you said, but it was very difficult. He did not want anything. He does not want to drink. He does not want to eat anything.' Her voice trembled.

The boy began to cough. Iyanla watched him closely and put her head on his little chest to listen. Then she rummaged in her basket and handed Kikelomo a small bundle tied in a cloth.

'This is a herbal pad,' she said. 'In it are agbo leaves, pawpaw leaves and other herbs. Just before he falls asleep in the evening, put the whole bundle in boiling water and let him breathe in the steam. Wrap the package in several towels, so that it is not too hot, and put it on his chest. First check on your own chest before you place it on his.'

Iyanla also handed her a small bottle of dark liquid. 'You give that to him three times over the day. But he has to eat something first. A little soup is enough. He has a sore throat and therefore eating will be uncomfortable for him.'

Kikelomo nodded, visibly relieved, and thanked her many times. 'My husband will come to see you tonight. He will bring something from the hunt,' she said. She took out four oranges from one of the baskets on the ground beside them and gave them to Simi. 'They're for you,' she said shyly.

Simi took them, surprised. 'Thank you,' she said.

Kikelomo smiled. 'It is an honour for me to meet Iyanla's granddaughter.'

Simi felt her cheeks burn in embarrassment, but thanked her again.

In the second house, they met a large woman working in the garden. She got up painfully from her knees, huffing and puffing, her forehead covered with sweat. She was about the same age as Iyanla and greeted her with a firm hug. They were obviously good friends. The woman also hugged Simi lavishly, pressing her to her large bosom. And when Iyanla introduced Simi as her granddaughter, she hugged her three times more.

'Oh, that I may experience this day,' she kept on saying. 'After all that happened and after Biola went away like that and we did not hear anything for years. Oh, that I should experience this day!' She hugged Simi twice more. 'I am Mama Ayoola,' she said. 'My daughter Ayoola and your mother played together as children. If Ayoola were here, she would be so happy to see you!'

Mama Ayoola was warm and open, had a loud voice and obviously liked to laugh. She was the opposite of Iyanla, who was small and wiry and calm. The two women spoke for a while before Iyanla made to leave. Before they did, Mama Ayoola brought a small roll of pretty cloth from the house.

'For you,' she said, hugging Simi one last time. 'I will send my granddaughter Bubu to come and keep you company. I never know where that girl is! But I am sure she will be happy to make a new friend.'

Simi was very surprised by the generous gift and thanked her several times. She put the smooth fabric alongside the oranges in her basket. It was a light green ankara fabric with a red floral pattern and it was really lovely. She would ask her mother to take her to the tailor so she could get a beautiful dress sewn with it.

After visiting a pregnant woman and a very old man with a skin rash on his back, Simi thought they were through with the visits. But Iyanla apparently went in everywhere to greet people briefly. Simi wondered if she always did that, or if she was doing it to introduce her granddaughter. Some people were at home or were preparing to go to the market to sell goods. The men were mostly not there. They had all left early to go to their farms.

All the villagers were very friendly and they seemed very calm, whereas in Lagos everyone always seemed to be in a rush. When they heard that Simi was the granddaughter of Iyanla, they showered her with good wishes and gifts. She was treated like a special guest. Simi received a lovely handcrafted fan, some bananas, a small shekere decorated with pearls to make music with, and three large yams, though she had to leave the yams, since they were too heavy to carry. The woman promised to send her son over in the evening with them.

'Now we can go home,' Iyanla said at last.

Simi was relieved because her basket was now quite heavy. They had been in every house in the village, except for one.

Simi thought that maybe Iyanla had forgotten the house because it was built away from the street. A long, bushy path led to it. The bushes looked as if they had once been planted with care but were now neglected. The path had not been swept in a while and there were leaves, old plastic bags and even a dead rat.

'Are we not going there?' Simi asked.

Just at that moment, a man came out of the house pushing a rusty bicycle. Simi recognized him at once. It was the unfriendly man with the yellowish eyes from the forest. He was wearing the same ragged clothes and his hair looked rough. To her relief, Iyanla shook her head and continued walking. When the man cycled past them, Iyanla nodded her head but the man ignored her and they did not greet each other.

'Who was that man?' Simi whispered when he was out of sight. 'And why did we not go in to see him?'

Iyanla did not reply right away.

When Simi almost thought that there would be no answer, she spoke, sounding thoughtful and sad, 'The backs of some people, like cats, never touch sand,' she said. 'Others may fall on their backs but will manage to get up and dust off the sand. But there are some who unfortunately get stuck and never manage to find their way up again.'

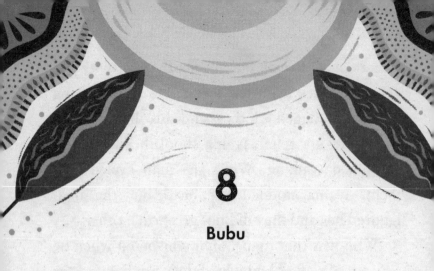

8

Bubu

When they arrived home, Simi fell exhausted on to the sofa bed in the little living room. But not even five minutes later, Iyanla called for her.

'Lunch rarely cooks itself on its own,' she said.

Simi groaned softly to herself but quickly went out into the yard.

Iyanla had put a bowl on the table. 'The rice needs to be cleaned,' she said.

Simi took the rice bowl to the iron buckets and was about to pour water into it to wash it when Iyanla stopped her.

'The rice must first be cleaned of stones and sand!' she said. 'Here we do not have the fine-fine ready-to-cook rice like you city people. Have you never prepared ofada rice?'

Simi shook her head. Iyanla looked at her with some resignation. She showed Simi how to sieve the rice and spread it out on the tabletop, how to take little portions and search them for stones, bits of leaves or dirt. It turned out to be a really boring job. It was even worse than hanging up piles of wet clothes that her mum had taken out of the washing machine or ironing her school uniform!

'I'm going to get efo leaves,' Iyanla said. 'When you're done, wash the rice and put it on the fire.'

Simi glanced at the hearth, hesitating.

'Have you ever made a fire?'

'No, I'm sorry,' Simi said, feeling useless.

'Hmm, I see, we still have a lot to learn, then.' Iyanla placed her hands on her narrow hips and looked uncertainly at the hearth. 'OK,' she said. 'Just clean the rice and wash it. I won't be long. When I get back, I will show you how to make a fire.'

Simi went into the house to search for the old-fashioned CD Walkman that her mum had given her for the trip. At first, when her mum handed it to her, smiling proudly at having found it in some old box, Simi had looked at the bulky, ancient-looking thing sceptically. But now, after checking her phone for the third time since her arrival and confirming that there was no sign of network and that it was officially dead, she was so grateful to have the CD player. She put on the headphones and began to clean the rice while bouncing her head to her mum's nineties' hip-hop. She became so absorbed in the task that after a while she had to stop to stretch her back. When she straightened up, she got a terrible fright. Two large round eyes were staring down at her from between the frangipani leaves.

She jumped up from the chair as a shy grin appeared. It belonged to a small, round girl with upright threaded braids, who swung down from the tree somewhat awkwardly. She wore a dress made of blue ankara that was slightly too tight around the belly. She looked about ten years old.

'Hi, what's your name?' Simi asked, pulling the headphones off her ears and letting them dangle around her neck.

The girl did not respond. She just stared, and

Simi realized she was staring at her headphones.

'Would you like to listen to my music?' Simi asked.

The girl nodded.

'If you tell me your name, I'll let you listen.'

The girl glared. She was fully aware that this was blackmail.

Simi grinned and winked, and the girl relaxed.

'Bubu,' she said in an unusually deep voice.

Simi tried not to laugh. The combination of this little, round person, the upright braids, deep voice and the name was so cute. Without a word, she handed Bubu the Walkman and headphones.

Bubu grabbed them as if she was afraid that Simi would change her mind. She slipped the headphones on, widened her eyes at Salt-N-Pepa's rap and seated herself at the table. She immediately set to work, picking clean the rice that Simi had abandoned. Simi sat opposite her and for a while they worked together in silence.

Simi caught Bubu staring at her every now and then but pretended not to notice. After a while Bubu took off the headphones.

'They say you are the daughter of Iyanla's

long-lost daughter.'

Simi nodded.

'They say it is good you have come home.'

Simi shrugged.

'You come from a big place?'

Simi nodded. 'Lagos.'

'Do you like our small place here?'

Simi nodded slowly. 'Yes . . . but it is very different, though. Some things are new and strange for me.'

'Oh, yes,' Bubu said, her voice falling to a whisper. 'This place is very different and strange!' She turned to glance at the forest behind the house. 'We have strange-strange things in Ajao. Magic things.'

'In the forest?' Simi asked, remembering her mum's letter and hoping she might get some more information from Bubu.

Bubu nodded her head vigorously. 'The forbidden lake!' she whispered. Then she held a finger to her lips and lowered her voice even more. 'We do not speak about magic things after midday. And after four o'clock we do not speak at all.'

Simi had to lean closer to hear her. 'Who made that rule?'

'Bubu's rule of survival,' the girl replied. 'And it works!' She touched the ground with her index finger, then she held it to her lips, licked the dust on the finger and pointed it up to the sky. 'I swear!' Her face was dead serious. 'May the god of thunder strike me down if I am lying.'

'Well, there's no need for anybody to strike anybody down,' Simi said. 'I believe you if you say that your rule of survival works for you.'

'They say that is how my mother disappeared.'

Simi looked up sharply. 'Oh, I am sorry to hear that.'

Bubu did not look at her but continued as if Simi had not said anything. 'She was talking about evil spirits at night in our backyard and a python swallowed her.'

'Oh my goodness! A python? Are you serious?' Simi asked.

Bubu nodded. 'I mean, who talks about evil spirits at night anyway?'

Simi did not know what to reply. 'So you live with your dad now?'

Bubu shook her head. 'I live with my grand-mother, Mama Ayoola.'

'Oh, yes, I remember. I met Mama Ayoola today and she mentioned you. She is a friendly woman,' Simi said with a smile, remembering the many hugs she had received.

Bubu grinned. But a moment later the smile left her face. 'I have not seen my father in a year now.' She had lowered her voice again. 'I think the bushbaby got him.'

Simi raised an eyebrow. 'What?'

'There was a time the bushbaby always cried behind our house at night, which made my father angry. Many things made him angry here. That we didn't have enough money, that my mother left him, that the farms did not give good harvest.'

Her mother left him? Simi thought. Didn't Bubu just say she got swallowed by a snake? But Bubu continued and so Simi just nodded.

'So one day, after he had a quarrel with my grandmother, he left to find a job and has not come back since. I told him not to go at night!' She bit her index finger with regret and then snapped her fingers.

'What is a bushbaby?'

'You mean you don't know bushbaby?' Bubu shook her head indignantly. 'He is a mean animal of the night. My biology teacher in school calls him galago, but we all know his name is bush-baby. He cries like an abandoned baby in need of help. But it is a trick.'

Simi made a note to research information on the galagos when next she had Wi-Fi.

Bubu looked around fearfully again. Then she rolled her eyes impatiently. 'What time is it?'

Simi looked at her watch. 'Two-thirty.'

'It is enough. I have spoken too much today.' Bubu traced a circle in the air above her head with her right hand and snapped her fingers. 'God forbid bad thing,' she mumbled to herself. Then she picked up the headphones and fitted them between her spiky braids. She adjusted her dress and continued picking the rice.

'But maybe your dad is busy trying to find a job somewhere else. Maybe he just hasn't had time to come back yet,' Simi said.

Bubu did not reply. She just shook her head. And even though Simi made several efforts to get her to say something, Bubu ignored her until Iyanla came back.

'Ah, Bubu. You kept Simi company?' Iyanla

asked when Bubu greeted her wordlessly with a dip of her knees.

Bubu nodded.

'Is it already too late in the day to speak?' Iyanla asked, as Bubu made to leave with a wave.

Simi waved goodbye to Bubu with a grin, then showed Iyanla the cleaned rice.

When the heat of the day slowly began to release everything from its sweaty grip, Simi had the feeling that she had completed survival training.

She had learnt how to make a fire and put a three-legged pot on it without getting burnt, how to draw water from a well with a rubber pouch on a long line without falling in, how to grind fresh tomatoes on a large flat stone with a small rounded stone, how to scrub the soot off the bottom of a pot with soap and sand, and how to cut yam into thin slices and spread them on a cloth under the sun to dry.

She groaned and wiped the sweat from her forehead when Iyanla told her the plans for the next days. She was going to show her how to make the traditional black soap, how to cook ewa agoyin and how to make ori body cream out of the shea nut. The only relief was that tomorrow they would be going to a nearby town – Ekita – to visit the chief of the area, so at least there would be one day of rest before the work continued.

'Did Bubu's mother really get swallowed by a python?' Simi asked as they sat in the backyard cracking pods again.

Iyanla looked up at Simi. 'Is that what she said?'

Simi nodded.

Iyanla shook her head. 'Her parents moved to one of those big-big cities to earn money. They have been gone for a year now. Bubu has missed her parents a lot and has found it difficult to understand why they couldn't take her with them. Mama Ayoola thinks that is why she keeps making up stories about how her parents died. Mama Ayoola has written a letter to Bubu's mother to tell her to come home, but Bubu does not believe they will come back.'

'That is sad!' Simi said.

Iyanla nodded. 'It is sad when parents are separated from their children.'

An awkward moment passed as Iyanla stared at the bowl of black beans in front of her.

Simi decided to change the topic and asked what had been on her mind all day. 'Bubu mentioned a forbidden lake in the forest,' she said slowly. 'Why is it forbidden? Is that the place Mum was talking about in her letter?'

She bit her lip as she realized she had brought the topic right back to her mum.

'Ah, Bubu and her mouth!' Iyanla said. She bent over her basin and scooped up more pods. 'It is a long story,' she said, 'and it is late.'

'I'm not tired at all and if the story is that long, I have two months to listen to you.'

The hint of a smile flickered over Iyanla's face. 'Well, on one condition! You have to promise to stay away from the lake and from the forest. There is a reason why it is forbidden to go there. Many have gone there and never returned.'

Simi shivered as she realized that she was probably extremely lucky to be sitting there right now.

'I am waiting for your answer,' Iyanla said.

'Yes! I promise to stay away from the forbidden lake.'

And I definitely will, she thought with a shudder.

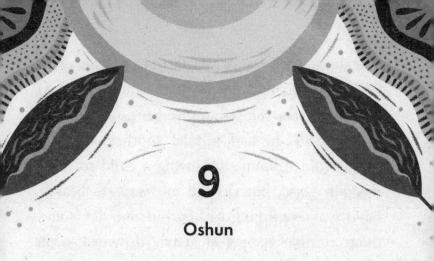

9

Oshun

Without a word, Iyanla pushed the bowl across the table towards Simi, who began helping to shell the little beans. Both of them had made a big pile of black pods before Iyanla found the right words and finally began to speak.

'It was a very long time ago,' she began in a low voice. 'The time when the gods and goddesses were still very close to the humans. There lived a woman called Adunni. She had a son, Layo, whom she loved above all else.'

Simi sat upright. *Layo*. The children in that strange quicksands place had mentioned Layo. It was not a common name.

Iyanla continued, 'Adunni loved Layo so much

that she swore never to give birth to another child. She said she could not imagine sharing her love for him. So she refused to give her husband other children, and he had to take another wife. The people told Adunni that loving a child so much was not good, but she did not want to hear it. Layo was everything to her. But one day something terrible happened. Layo drowned while playing in a lake.'

At the mention of a lake, Simi felt her palms become sweaty.

Iyanla's eyes were distant and turned towards the forest. 'Adunni was a broken woman. She refused to eat and mourned for months on end. She went to the lake and prayed to Oshun, goddess of the rivers and waters. She prayed for seven days and seven nights without eating. The goddess did not answer. But Adunni did not give up.

'She made a vow to Oshun that she would weep seven calabashes full of tears into the lake every day for the rest of her life if Oshun returned her son to her. She went to the lake every day and cried seven calabashes of tears. On the seventh day, Oshun finally took pity. She went to her sister, Oya, goddess of the winds and also guardian of the gate to the Egun – the dead. Oshun asked her to allow the boy to return from the dead. Oya refused. "Bringing back the dead will only cause problems and is not the way of things."

'But Oshun was relentless and Oya reconsidered the case for several days. Finally, because of her love for her sister she agreed to Oshun's request, though very reluctantly.'

Iyanla paused and sighed, as if the story were real.

'Adunni was overjoyed to have her son back and she thanked Oshun joyously. She came to the lake every day as promised and wept seven calabashes full of tears of joy and gratitude. But after a while Adunni forgot the pain of the loss. She cried less, no longer filling the calabashes with tears, and one day she stopped coming to the lake.

'Oshun became very angry, because it had cost her much persuasion to bring Layo back from the land of the Egun. She raged, angry at Adunni's lack of gratitude, and swelled up the river near the village where Adunni lived. She stormed the village with her waters and swept Layo along with her. Adunni, who could not bear to lose him a second time, jumped into the floods and drowned herself in order to be with her son.

'But when Oshun arrived at the gates of the Egun with Layo, Oya refused to take the boy back. "We do not take the same person twice. The dead ones should not begin to think they can walk in and out of this place as they please," she said.

'Oshun was very, very angry. She threw wave upon wave of water over the lands. But Oya thrust heavy winds against the waters and held them back with a wall of her winds. The sisters quarrelled for days and the whole land was in trouble and suffered many deaths.

'At last, Oshun left. She could not return the boy to the living, so she decided to banish Layo to a huge bubble underneath the same lake in which he had drowned the first time. She whirled the waters of the lake around until she had created a world for him and then pushed the boy inside.

'But Layo looked at her with sad eyes and her heart softened, because Oshun has a big heart for children. So she created a beautiful world for him.

And when Layo asked her what he should eat there, she pushed plants and animals into the bubble. And when he asked what he should drink, she let little streams flow in. And when he asked whom he should talk to, she told him that she would leave open a tiny passage. A place where the sand on the banks of the lake could give way. And once every ten years, a child of Oshun would find its way there. The child would sink into the quicksands of the lake and slip into the bubble, never to return. It would join Layo and become his playmate.

'After that Oshun turned her back on him and closed the bubble for ever.'

There was silence. Simi found she could hardly breathe.

Iyanla nodded, slowly turning to look at Simi. Her eyes were piercing and her expression grave. 'Ever since, every ten years, a child disappears at the forbidden lake and never comes home, reminding us of what happened.'

Simi was so shocked that her legs had begun to tremble, making some beans fall off the table. Her thoughts scrambled wildly through her brain.

This world – this bubble under the quicksand – it was definitely the place she had been in her vivid dream. She had seen it, with its strange, quivering red hills. And the two boys had mentioned the name Layo.

She did not understand anything any more. She couldn't have actually been there, since no one ever came back. But how come she had dreamt of it? Was it because the lake was magical? Had the lake somehow connected with her? Was that why she had imagined being down there? But it had all felt so real, and she had seen those children and definitely heard them! She felt panic rise within her and had to take a deep breath.

'Is everything all right?' Iyanla asked, and she realized that her grandmother was watching her closely.

'Yes, of course,' Simi said, trying to hide her fright with a smile. But deep inside her she didn't feel all right at all.

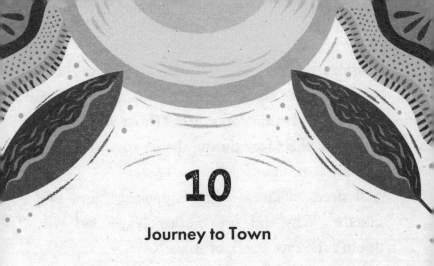

10

Journey to Town

It was still dark when Simi awoke the next morning. She hadn't slept well. She remembered terrible dreams in which she was whirled around in red quicksand. She had struggled, but the sands had not released her. They had teased and tortured her, only freeing her head for tiny moments, just long enough for her to gasp for breath, then pulling her back inside. She felt as if she had spent the whole night fighting for her life. Every part of her body felt sore.

At breakfast she felt Iyanla's sharp gaze on her. 'It appears the spirits of the dream world did not leave you in peace last night,' she murmured.

Simi nodded dejectedly and poked at her

porridge.

'The spirits come to those who are afraid of something,' Iyanla continued. 'Those who do not deal with their fear during the day are visited by the spirits at night.'

'I need to know what happened,' Simi said quietly. 'Why did my mother leave and why doesn't she ever speak of Ajao?'

Iyanla turned her gaze away and stared into the distance. At first she looked thoughtful, then a shadow darkened her eyes.

'Let us go and come first,' she said. 'Then we will see. Eat now, my child. We have a long march ahead of us to Ekita. It is better we get there before sunrise, otherwise we are lost to the heat.'

The journey was indeed long. Simi, who was not used to walking long distances, was already exhausted after an hour's fast march. They had first walked on the main road but now they were on a shortcut through farmland and dry-looking fields. Her shoulder hurt because of the heavy basket she carried. The sun was beginning to rise and it was getting warmer. She thought longingly of the motorbike that had passed them previously on the main road.

'Didn't Kikelomo's husband have an okada?' she asked Iyanla. 'Why didn't we ask him for a ride?' One of the villagers had mentioned that Kikelomo's husband ran a taxi business in the village with his motorbike, driving the villagers when they needed to go to town.

'As far as I can see, our legs are strong and well,' Iyanla replied dryly. Simi sighed and hurried to catch up with her.

To her surprise, she had trouble keeping up with Iyanla. Her little grandmother marched forward as if she had an engine propelling her. Iyanla carried her own basket on her head. She had rolled a cloth into a snake-like rope and twisted it into a snail-shell as protection for her head and as a solid base for the basket. She had not even bothered asking Simi if she knew how to balance a basket on her head but had handed her a little basket with a handle to sling over her arm.

'The children from our village walk this path every day to get to school,' Iyanla called over her shoulder. 'If they walked as slowly as you, they would miss half of the lessons.'

Simi groaned and tried to walk faster. Meanwhile, the sweat was running down her body in little streams. *Gosh*, she thought. *Poor kids! Every day!* Her mum dropped her off at school every morning. She didn't even have to take a bus! Well, at least the children only walked this journey during the week, she thought. But, as if Iyanla had guessed her thoughts, her grandmother said: 'And on Sunday, they walk this way again to go to church to worship the god of the white man.'

Simi rolled her eyes. Who still called church 'the white man's church'? The colonial era in which the British had taken over the land and the white missionaries had converted the people had ended sixty years ago. There were no more white missionaries in any churches. But she did not say anything. She lacked the strength and the breath to speak anyway.

To her immense relief, they arrived in Ekita shortly afterwards. The bush path led out on to a tarmac road, not a red sandy road with potholes. Simi saw a supermarket, a post office, a little restaurant, office buildings and a larger building with the sign 'town hall'. Cars drove past and busy people walked by. A large football field sat behind a pale-yellow building that was clearly a school but empty because of the holidays.

It was not a big town, not even close to Lagos, but compared to remote Ajao, it seemed so alive, with its pylons and power cables criss-crossing over colourful houses and busy roads.

Simi looked at everything wide-eyed. 'It is great here!' she said to Iyanla. 'It's all, so . . .'

'New?' Iyanla asked with raised eyebrows, and Simi felt a little ashamed about her excitement.

'Erm . . . well . . . different from Ajao.'

Iyanla did not reply.

After a short moment, Simi had to ask: 'Why do you live so far away from everything?'

'Ajao is our home,' Iyanla said. 'It is the land of our ancestors and their ancestors before them.'

'Yes, but . . .'

'Not everyone sees the fine-fine new things as the answer for everything,' Iyanla interrupted her. 'We are happy with the small that we have. We may have no electricity and no cars and TV, but we have fewer problems. We do not have to borrow; we have always had enough food for our mouths and clothes for our bodies. We do not have to look for jobs and worry about tomorrow. We work the lands the way our parents did and may not have plenty, but we are happy. Maybe not everyone, I admit. Many young people have left for the big cities. But those of us who have stayed do not need your pity. We are happy where we are.'

Now Simi felt truly ashamed and hid her face by staring at the ground as they marched along the road.

'So, we have arrived,' Iyanla said, stopping abruptly in her tracks.

They stood in front of a large white house, partially hidden behind a high wall. Iyanla knocked on the metal gate, and it echoed loudly. A thin man in a long black caftan and a turban opened it for them instantly.

He bowed his head deeply when he saw Iyanla and moved aside to let her in. They walked through a large courtyard, where several cars were parked, and along a path that led to the house. The front door was made of a dark brown wood and decorated with intricate carvings. A lion with a huge proud mane looked down at his subjects. The subjects were humans and looked up at him in awe.

The man in the turban hurried past them and opened the door. Only then did Iyanla lower her basket from her head. The man led her through a hall, into a room where a number of people appeared to be waiting.

Most were men wearing suits, traditional caftans or agbadas made of expensive fabrics. The two women present wore artfully bound, glittering geles on their heads. Simi immediately felt wrong in her plain dark-blue dress and dusty sandals. Iyanla, with her simple wrapper and matching blouse, did not seem worried about their appearance and sat down on one of the four long benches that lined the walls. A fan above their heads made swishing noises. Simi shyly mumbled a quiet good morning before she sat down beside Iyanla. The people looked at her curiously. They greeted Iyanla or smiled at her as if they knew her.

Simi was just enjoying the breeze of the fan and

resting her tired feet when the door at the far end of the room was flung open. A man stomped out, mumbling angrily. Simi recognized the ragged man from the forest. Every time she had seen him, he had seemed to be in a bad mood. Everyone in the room stared after him, and one of the women shook her head and looked sad.

The thin man in the turban hurried into the room. 'Iyanla! The chief will receive you now,' he said in his deep voice.

Iyanla got up, picked up her basket and followed him, while Simi was still thinking about the ragged man and wondering why they were called in before all the other people who had been here first.

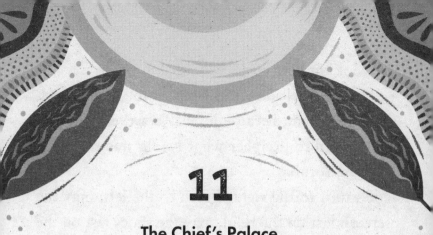

11

The Chief's Palace

Simi and Iyanla were shown into a large hall, which was lavishly furnished. Golden sofas with ornate armrests and backrests, and colourful carpets adorned the room. Wooden sculptures stood tall between the furniture, and carvings hung on the walls among portraits of one and the same man. And, at the far end, sitting in a big chair, was the man himself.

He was wearing a light-grey caftan with exquisite silver embroidery at the neck and wrists. His arms were spread out on the armrests of his chair, giving him a majestic look. Simi felt shy and out of place. She was not sure if she should have come in here at all. Iyanla had not even turned around to look for her.

Iyanla knelt down in front of the man, which surprised Simi because he was not even that old. Simi tried to decipher what Iyanla was saying to him in Yoruba.

'I turn to the right, I turn to the left, may the crown last on the head, may the shoes last on the feet. May the irukere be strong in the hand, and the authority strong in the mouth, the food plenty on the plate. Hail the king, second in command to the Orisha.'

The man smiled warmly at Iyanla and made a sign that she should come closer. 'It's been a long time since we saw the priestess of the goddess Oshun inside of these walls. We are honoured with her presence.' He gestured to a little sofa beside his chair. 'Please have your seat, great Iyanla. And thank you for your gifts.'

'Chief, it is with pleasure in my heart to see you as young and strong as always.'

'I hear it is rare for anybody to see the priestess anywhere outside Ajao nowadays.'

'Forgive an old woman, chief. It is old age and lack of interest in the tiresome politics of the young people nowadays that keeps me at home.'

The chief did not respond to this. 'Surprisingly, you brought someone with you, but the person does not dare to come closer,' he said instead.

Simi jerked up and felt her heart beat wildly. Was he talking about her?

The chief raised his arm and stuck his nose into his caftan. 'Maybe I do not smell so good today? Maybe that is why she does not come closer than ten steps?' He winked at Iyanla as he spoke and Simi, who stood frozen at the end of the room, awoke from her stupor and ran forward. She stopped and bent her knees so abruptly in front of him that she fell awkwardly to the ground.

'Ekaaro, sir,' she gasped, hoping that her simple good morning was respectful enough for a chief.

'And does this adorable person have a name?' he asked.

'Simi,' she answered. 'My name is Oluwanifesimi, sir, erm, Your Honour. I mean, Your Highness? Your Chiefness?'

'This is my granddaughter.' Iyanla interrupted Simi's rambling, to her great relief. 'She came to see me from Lagos.'

The chief sat up. 'Show me your face, child,' he said.

Simi looked at him and now saw that he actually had a very friendly face. He had a broad, prominent chin, but his big, light-brown eyes were soft. At the temples, peeking out from his fila, were a few grey hairs.

'So, this is the daughter of Biola!' the chief said and a slightly thoughtful, almost sad look came over his face. 'She does not seem very talkative?' he said to Iyanla. 'Unlike her mother.' Now his eyes took on a brighter gleam and he grinned.

Simi thought for a moment if she should say something, but she could not think of anything important enough to say in front of a chief.

'Biola did not come.' The chief said it like a statement, not a question.

'No,' Iyanla replied. 'I was surprised that she sent me her daughter.'

'That is a pity. I would have loved to see her. She was such a free spirit, and a great dancer,' he said thoughtfully, touching the thick coral beads around his neck.

Simi placed her basket beside Iyanla's and

quickly seated herself next to her grandmother on the little sofa. The chief's words – *free spirit, great dancer* – shot like needles through her belly. Obviously this chief had known her mum well.

Why did it seem as if everyone knew her mother better than she did? Her mum had clearly been a totally different person when she lived here as Iyanla's daughter. What had happened to her?

She looked at Iyanla from the corner of her eyes. Her grandmother never ceased to surprise her. Why had the chief called her the *priestess of the goddess Oshun*? Had he meant it as a joke? She tried to remember the story that Iyanla had told her. It was Oshun who had banished the little boy into the bubble under the lake – the goddess of the waters.

'Iyanla, it is good that you have come,' the chief went on. 'Sooner or later, I would have sent for you. I assume you saw Baba Morayo just now?'

Iyanla nodded and Simi realized he meant the ragged man.

'He comes here every week since his daughter, Morayo, disappeared three months ago,' the chief said. 'He seeks justice that I cannot give him. He says his daughter should not have been taken. That it was not the time. And he is right. Why has the goddess begun to take more children? Iyanla, Priestess of Oshun, I ask you?'

Simi, who had been caught up in her own thoughts, began listening closely to their conversation. She could almost feel her ears grow. The chief had to be talking about the forbidden lake and the story of Layo. What did he mean by Oshun taking more children than usual?

'Chief, I do not know,' Iyanla replied. Her voice was quiet and she blinked uneasily. 'It is not her way. Are we sure that the child really went to Oshun's lake? Maybe it is something else?'

The chief shook his head. 'The last person to set eyes on her saw her entering the forest. And apart from that, how should anyone just disappear? And to where should they disappear? There are no secrets around here. If a person farts in his house in the morning, by nightfall everybody will know about it.'

'Yes, you are right. It is strange. And it worries me,' Iyanla said. Her forehead had creased and she stared into the distance.

'But do you know what worries me even more are the increasingly loud voices among my advisers. My brother and his followers are putting a lot of pressure on me.'

Simi felt Iyanla stiffen beside her. 'What do you mean?' she said.

'They want to fill up Oshun's lake and sell the land for farming.'

'You are not serious about this?' Iyanla asked sharply.

Simi, who had sat still and kept her head lowered, looked up at the chief. He did not reply, only raised his eyebrow meaningfully.

'Chief, with all due respect, this is not your land to touch or sell.' Iyanla's voice was very cold now. 'The lake and the land around it are sacred and belong to Oshun. Who touches them should be ready to face her wrath.'

The chief raised his hand. 'I have not said that I agree with them. I am just telling you what the voices of my people are saying. The people will feel safer if we fill up the lake and end this business once and for all.'

Iyanla got up. 'It is not our place to end it.' Her

small figure was stiff. 'It will be our downfall if we touch that lake.'

Now the chief stood up as well. He looked anxiously from Iyanla to Simi, then he called loudly: 'Moktar!'

The thin man with the turban came in.

'Please bring our young guest here to see Jide.' He winked at Simi. 'My son will be glad to receive a visitor from the city. And this is no place for your tender ears,' he added, before turning back to Iyanla.

Simi got up and walked slowly to the door, where the thin man was waiting for her. She was annoyed. Now she definitely did not want to leave. But of course she did not dare argue. Her legs carried her unwillingly, and she tried to listen to the quiet voice of the chief behind her as she left.

'The people are tired of being weighed down by this old myth. Many doubt that the gods and goddesses are still interested in us. Some do not even believe in them any more. They say that the lake is only dangerous due to the quicksands. That there is nothing true about the story. They say it is a story for a moonlit night around a fire.'

'He who wants to do what no one has ever done should be ready to see what no one has ever seen.' Simi heard Iyanla's voice, hard and threatening, just before Moktar closed the door behind her.

Moktar led Simi out into a beautiful garden enclosed by four houses. A paved path adorned with well-tended shrubs led to a large circular space in the middle, where a cashew tree sheltered a few comfortable-looking bamboo chairs.

The houses were built in colonial style, with sloping roofs and long verandas, each one painted a different colour. Moktar headed for a bright green one, where someone was standing on the veranda. It was a boy who looked roughly her own age, maybe a little older, wearing cool ripped jeans, white trainers and a white polo shirt. He looked very neat and stylish. The white trainers gleamed and showed no signs of dust. His face was hidden behind a pair of sunglasses, and he was obviously trying to get a signal because he was holding a mobile phone stretched out in front of him and was moving carefully in a circle.

'Mr Jide,' Moktar said. 'There is a guest for you.' He tilted his head in Simi's direction and walked away.

'I am not his guest!' she called, totally embarrassed. 'I . . . I just got sent . . .' But Moktar had gone.

She turned to the boy. He had said nothing yet, just kept looking at his phone. She stood there, feeling very stupid and out of place. She cleared her throat nervously.

'Hi,' he said at last, putting his phone in his back pocket. He sounded bored.

Simi once again regretted not having worn something other than her simple dark-blue dress. And the dusty roads had transformed her sandals and feet into two reddish-brown clouds of dust.

She felt ashamed but at the same time annoyed about being forced into this weird situation.

'You know what, don't mind me. I don't want to bother anybody,' she said. 'I can wait somewhere until my grandmother is ready. It was your father who sent me to you.' She knew she was being childish, but she did not care. This chief's son was not going to look down on her.

'And who are you?' The boy seemed unimpressed.

'Simi.'

'Aha!'

'Well, then, like I said, your father is talking to my grandmother about a sacred lake right now and I guess I was probably in the way.' She took a step back. 'I'll wait under the tree over there.'

But he followed her and there was an uncomfortable silence.

Simi sat down beneath the tree, glad of the shade.

'Well, you're not from here, that's for sure,' he said, switching to English.

Simi eyed him without answering.

'Are you just here for the holidays?'

'Yes, I'm from Lagos.'

'Aha! I almost thought so. And you wanted to get some country air here in Ekita?'

'I did not come here to smell any country air!' Simi said, annoyed. 'My parents have no time during the holidays, and that's why I had to come here. And my grandmother does not live in Ekita, but in Ajao.'

'You seem to be often "in the way" and sent elsewhere.' He grinned cheekily.

She glared at him, feverishly thinking of a snappy response. But, of course, she couldn't think of one.

'Wait, did you just say your grandma is from Ajao and she's meeting my father about the lake?' He looked at her curiously.

'Yes. My grandmother – Iyanla – comes from Ajao.'

He looked at her in disbelief, then threw his head back and laughed. He pushed up his sunglasses and Simi saw he had the same soft brown eyes as his father.

'You! You are the granddaughter of the old priestess of Oshun? How awesome is that!'

She glared at him. 'What do you mean?'

'Well, it's hilarious. You're a city kid, an ajebutter.' He was grinning even more now.

'I am not a pampered butter child!' Simi answered hotly. 'You do not know me at all. I'm not jumping to conclusions about you just because you're wearing your white Ralph Laurens or whatever. I mean, for goodness' sake, who wears white shoes in such a dusty place?'

He got up, tilting his head. 'Ah, ah? You mean you don't like my style?'

Simi snorted and folded her arms. 'That is not the point! You can't just put me in a box like that.'

'Hey, I was just joking, OK!' he said, holding up his hands. 'It was the way you were so annoyed about being sent out here, like you were too cool to hang out with the likes of me. And then that English accent in your Yoruba, so obviously city kid.'

Now he had really made her angry. She hated that her Yoruba was not perfect. 'You know what? I do not have to stand here and let myself be put down by you. I am sorry for the disturbance.' She got up and marched away angrily, feeling like she needed a punch bag.

'Hey, Simi! I was just joking!' He sounded sorry, but she did not turn. She would rather stay in the waiting room until Iyanla was finished than hang around with that idiot for one more minute.

Even later that night, when she was in bed, she was still angry with him. Although she realized that she might actually have sounded a bit snappy when she was left standing in front of him and he'd ignored her. But that did not give him the right to make fun of her!

And she was annoyed with Iyanla as well. On the way home she had tried everything possible to learn more about the conversation between her and the chief, but Iyanla had not said a word about it.

'It was the curiosity of the cat that got her paws burning with hot pepper soup,' was all she'd had to say on the matter.

12

Jay

The next day they had just had lunch when they heard a loud motor at the front of the house. Then there was a knock on the front door. Simi was holding the palm-frond broom and sweeping up leaves under the frangipani tree.

'Come inside, or do you see a locked door?' Iyanla called.

When the chief's son appeared in front of them in the backyard, Simi wished she could sink into the ground or disappear into thin air. She had tied up her long braids into a large messy bun with an oversized batik cloth. She was barefoot and her feet were dusty red, but, worst of all, she was wearing her bright pink 'I-believe-in-unicorns' T-shirt.

The chief's son was wearing dark-grey jeans and a dark-blue T-shirt.

'Ekaason,' he greeted Iyanla respectfully and bowed his head deeply, while touching the ground with his hand.

'Ekaason, Jide, nice to see you, my son. Yesterday we did not have the opportunity to speak. You look more and more like your father. I'm sure the girls are already lining up at your father's gate to see you.'

'Iyanla, your words are kind,' he replied. 'How is your health?'

Iyanla rewarded him with a smile that Simi was almost jealous of. She obviously liked this boy.

'Are you going to eat something?' Iyanla asked. 'We just finished eating but we will sit down with you.'

'That's very kind of you, Iyanla, but I've already had breakfast with my father's two wives in a row and I'm about to burst. If this continues, I will soon only be able to wear shokotos with an elastic waist. Hello, Simi,' he said, turning to her. 'Nice T-shirt.'

'Hello,' she mumbled, then added, 'Excuse me,' and disappeared into the house.

She grabbed a rag and rubbed her feet clean, then slipped into her trainers.

Outside in the yard, she could hear Jide telling Iyanla that his father had sent him to tell her that she should attend a meeting of the elders of Ekita the following day.

Simi ran quickly into the living room, where her suitcase stood in the corner. She released her braids from the batik cloth and rummaged for a less childish T-shirt. She grabbed her plain green one with the cool oversize cut, then hurried into Iyanla's room to change, feeling stupid about being so bothered about what he thought.

She had never been in Iyanla's room before and did not know if it was actually OK to go in there. But she certainly wasn't planning to walk past Jide with the clothes in her hand to go and change in the shower shed at the back. And she did not want to change in the living room in case he or anyone else came in.

In Iyanla's room there was a narrow bed and a cupboard with a mirror and some old photos propped up next to it. But it was the strange little construction in one corner that froze her. It looked, at first glance, like a miniature version of a hut – a sort of doll's house, with two compartments and a thatched roof made of grass and palm fronds. The whole thing was perhaps a metre high and a metre wide and not so deep. She knelt down to look at the strange-looking things inside.

There was an intricately decorated bowl made of coconut shell filled with a thick golden-looking liquid that looked like honey. Next to it was a black fly whisk made of a cow's tail, and a long black feather that could have belonged to a vulture or an eagle. In the other compartment she saw four groups of four cowries, neatly arranged around a little rust-stained mirror. There was a small pile of fresh-looking river-grass like she had seen growing in the stream outside, and a few small wooden carvings placed on it. The wooden figures were stained dark red and she suddenly realized that it might be blood. This was obviously a shrine!

She edged away hastily, her heart pounding, and hurriedly changed her T-shirt. And, without looking in the direction of the shrine again, she rushed out of the room.

Outside, the guest was chatting with Iyanla as if they were old friends.

He turned towards her. 'My father also sent me to see you, Simi. He said I should take care of you and show you around.'

'That's very nice of your dad, but I do not need a village guide, thank you,' she replied.

'Ahn, ahn, Simi!' Iyanla admonished her. 'What has got into you?' Her brow was deeply furrowed. 'You should apologize to Jide.'

The boy raised his hands. 'No, no, it's my fault. Yesterday, I was not very welcoming to Simi. I'm really sorry for my bad manners. Can we start afresh?'

Simi hesitated, but under Iyanla's keen eye she had no choice. She shrugged. 'All right,' she said.

'Call me Jay,' he said, switching to English. 'That's what all my friends call me. Our country-side may look rather boring at first glance, especially for a . . . erm . . . city kid, but we do have a few spots that are worth checking out.' He grinned again, this time so broadly that she realized it was going to be difficult keeping up her stony face. She gave him a small smile.

117

'Tonight the drums will be calling from Ajao for old and young to come and dance. Maybe you would like to join us?' Iyanla asked him.

'Oh, I would like that,' Jay replied, smiling.

Iyanla nodded and returned to her mixture of grains, which she was grinding between two smooth stones. 'Enjoy yourselves,' she said.

Simi frowned. It felt strange going out and not having someone ask her where exactly she was going, when she would be back and warning her to be careful. She was also not at all sure about being taken around by Jay, though Iyanla obviously trusted him. But Jay was already heading for the door, so she said goodbye to Iyanla and went with him.

A goat jumped at their sudden appearance in the front yard and ran away, bleating loudly. Some chickens that were surprised by the goat panicked and flew in the air, scattering feathers. Simi ducked, holding her hands over her head.

When she looked up she saw Jay watching her with a smile tugging at his lips. Moktar was standing beside a car, also watching. She felt foolish.

'So where are you taking me?' she snapped.

'Wow, the other Lagos kids I know do not have such a sharp tongue!' Jay said, scratching his head and looking embarrassed.

Simi bit her lip, wishing she hadn't been so mean. He really seemed to be making an effort to be friendly. She decided to give him a chance.

'Are city kids afraid of adventures?' He had on his cheeky face again and Simi smiled slyly.

She folded her arms. 'Never underestimate city kids.'

He grinned. 'Then follow me.'

He exchanged a few words with Moktar, asking him to pick him up later that evening after the festival.

They headed down the main road, past the few Ajao houses and the curious stares of some little children kicking a football.

'Where exactly in Lagos do you come from? Mainland or island?' Jay asked.

'Mainland,' she replied, surprised that he seemed to know Lagos a bit. 'I live in Ikeja and go to school there too. Do you know Lagos? Have you been there before?'

He nodded. 'Awesome city.'

Simi recognized the path ahead as the one she had taken with Iyanla the day before.

'Are we going to Ekita?'

He shook his head. 'We will turn off the path and go uphill in that direction.' He pointed to green hills in the distance.

'Ekita is a much more happening place than Ajao. I mean, you guys even have a mobile phone network!' Simi said.

'Well, most of the time, actually, we don't have a network and are searching for it. But, yes, Ekita is all right. Is this your first ever visit to your grandmother's?'

'Yes.'

'Have you ever left Lagos before?'

'No,' she said uncomfortably, feeling some-what unworldly and naive.

'Wow! And then your first visit outside Lagos is to Ajao, of all places. That's tough!' he chuckled. 'Growing up here is great, though. I would never want another childhood,' he added.

They passed the last house and Jay turned off

the road and down the path that led to a wide expanse of farmland.

Simi looked back at Ajao. Two women were sitting in the shade of a large almond tree in front of the last house. They were chatting and laughing, babies playing at their feet. The children playing football were running around a red open space, chasing a tattered-looking ball. Most were sparsely clothed – a singlet over dusty shorts or just shorts – and were laughing and shouting. Other children stood beneath a large tree, holding up long sticks and calling to more children who were sitting in the tree.

She thought of her extremely protected childhood in Lagos. Driven to school in the morning and picked up by her mum in the afternoon. Then back home to learn. A bit of TV was allowed, a lot of reading, then a tutor or the piano teacher came. She was never allowed to go out to meet friends on her own.

When she wanted a play-date, she had to wait for the weekend. She was never allowed to hang out with the children in the neighbourhood. Her mum did not like them because they played

Nintendo and watched TV all day. And those who played football on the street were too rough, her mum said. She was not even allowed to go to the main street alone to buy chicken suya or plantain chips. That might have been all right with her dad, but her mum never allowed it. That had been one of the reasons for the constant arguments between her parents – the over-protectiveness of her mum. Wistfully, she looked at the children in the tree. If there had been such a big tree among all the huge concrete buildings in her neighbourhood, her mum would never have allowed her to climb it.

'The kids look like they're having fun here,' she said with a sigh.

'Yep,' Jay replied.

'So where are we going?' she asked after a while.

'I want to show you my favourite place, which I discovered as a kid. You said you are up for adventure, right?'

Simi smiled. She was actually beginning to enjoy herself.

13

King and Queen of the World

Simi and Jay soon turned on to a smaller path that curved between rows of trees and tall bushes. They began to talk about all sorts of things. About Davido's and Wizkid's music, about Nollywood, Bollywood and Hollywood films, and their best foods. Simi realized Jay was actually quite an interesting person to talk to and he was constantly making her laugh.

The landscape became more overgrown with fewer farms. But everything looked very dry and parched and the plants in the fields were yellow and scant. In one strange-looking farm, Simi saw piled-up mounds of earth and plants curling their tendrils around long sticks.

'Those plants look funny,' she said. 'Are they meant to be so yellow?'

'That's a yam farm,' he said.

'Oh, I have never seen yam growing before,' she said without thinking and, to her relief, he did not make fun of her.

'The farms are all dried out. The rains are extremely late. My dad says it's unnaturally hot and dry this year. The farmers are losing a lot of crops.'

Simi remembered Iyanla saying the goddesses Oya and Oshun were fighting and causing the drought. In Ajao the strangest of things seemed possible. Goddesses existed; they changed the weather when they quarrelled and took children through sacred lakes. She shook her head.

'It really is very hot!' she moaned, wiping sweat from her forehead and looking up at the bright sky.

The landscape slowly became hilly and rocks began to appear, jutting out in the middle of the bushes. It was all very different from the flat coastal land around Lagos, almost another world. Soon they were right in the forest. The air became damp and heavy. The sun came through the crowns of the trees in dispersed rays.

'Watch out for snakes,' Jay said.

'What?' she asked, startled.

'Well, we have a lot of poisonous snakes and scorpions in this region.'

Simi immediately scanned the path in front of her.

'They are probably resting away from the heat under a cool stone, but I would still be careful where I step.'

She suddenly remembered her first day here and how she had raced barefoot through the Ajao forest after her strange, scary dream. She shivered and pushed the thought away.

'Do you believe the story about the forbidden lake and the legend of Oshun and Layo?' she asked Jay.

'Wow, you already heard that story?'

'Iyanla told me.'

'Oh, right. Of course. I forgot,' he said, looking lost in thought. 'She had to warn you after what happened . . .' He broke off, and Simi wondered why he looked uncomfortable.

'So is the story true, you think?'

He seemed to be searching for words. 'I definitely know that children have disappeared there. And I know that the lake has probably been considered dangerous and forbidden for centuries. Of course, we went there as children and it did look quite peaceful and nice, but . . .'

'You played there as children?' Simi asked, startled.

'Well, we didn't actually play there. And we would never have dared to go too close. We just took a peek as a test of courage, and then ran away as fast as our short legs could carry us.'

'And has anyone ever been . . . down there and returned to tell the story?'

He shook his head. 'Well, that is the point of the whole story: that nobody ever comes back. Anyone who goes there is doomed to stay there and keep Layo company for ever.'

Simi thought again about her own experience. A shiver ran down her spine as if cold hands had just stroked her back. If she had dreamt it, how come it had felt so real? And how could she have dreamt of the place without ever having heard of it before? She shook her head as if to shake herself awake, and looked around, stopping to notice how the forest had changed. They had been marching uphill for a while now and she was slightly out of breath.

In front of them a huge rock blocked the view, towering higher than the treetops.

'Wow!' she whispered in awe.

'It is wow, isn't it?' Jay replied.

It was beautifully shaped. Smooth and impressive, like a giant's throne in the middle of the jungle. Even the trees seemed to arch towards the rock as if bowing their heads to it.

'Wait until we get to the top.'

'The top?' Simi felt dizzy from staring up. 'What do you mean?'

He didn't reply. She turned around and realized she was alone.

'Jay?' she called in sudden fear. Still no reply. Her heart began to thump loudly and she took a step away from the rock. How could he have disappeared so suddenly?

'Are you coming?' She heard Jay's voice from somewhere on the other side of the rock. She almost fainted with relief and immediately stumbled in that direction.

The path snaked around the rock and she ran quickly, only slowing down when she finally saw him waiting for her.

'What did you mean by "wait until we get to the top"?' A wild fluttering sound and a shriek spread out of the trees before a flock of birds did the same. She caught up with him and paused, puffing.

'If you keep shouting like that, we will have no nature left to see.' Jay grinned. 'You are scaring away every animal in a two-kilometre radius.'

'Oh, sorry.' She smiled sheepishly.

'When I was younger,' Jay said, 'my friends and I used to climb up the rock and play kings and queens of the world on the top. I have not been up there for ages, but I think we should be able to do it.'

It was not that difficult. In contrast to the smooth, sheer face of the rock, the back was like the long, gnarled roots of a tree, rising slowly, with enough bumps and edges for foot and hand holds, so they soon reached the top.

Simi could see for miles. It was such an exhilarating feeling that for a moment she was speechless. Far in the distance was a horizontal line where the greens of the forest ended and the reddish fields began. After that came the villages, with their mix of thatched and rusty metal roofs. And all around her, the treetops whispered mysteriously.

'I've never seen anything so beautiful,' she said after a while.

Jay lay down on the rock, face to the sky. She copied him. The sun was slowly on its way down now. Simi closed her eyes and let her thoughts fly, overwhelmed by a sudden rush of freedom. She felt absolutely free of worries, and no longer angry with her mum. She pushed her thoughts about the world under the lake away and just enjoyed the moment.

'It is being outside like this and feeling free that I miss most when I am in Lagos,' Jay said.

Simi sat up. 'When you are in Lagos? What do you mean by that?'

'I go to school there.'

'What?' Simi couldn't believe her ears.

He buckled with laughter now and she smacked his arm without even thinking.

'So I am a city kid and an ajebutter, heh? And all this while, you were hiding the fact that you are a Lagos kid as well?' Now she had to laugh, too.

'Not exactly like you, though! I only go to school there. I was born and raised in Ekita. I'm from here.' He pointed his finger to the rock and grinned.

'Oh, rubbish! I can't believe you fooled me like that. You're such a trickster,' she said, laughing. She lay back down. 'Are you in a boarding school, then?'

'Yes,' he said. 'After my mum died, my dad wanted it that way. His other wives would have taken me in, they have always been nice to me, but he wanted me to get away from here. He said I should see the world and then bring the world back to Ekita.' He paused. 'Whenever I sit up here, I always think that the people from Lagos should be the ones to come here. They should leave their daily traffic jams, packed markets and city-life stress, and see the world out here.'

'When did your mother die?' Simi asked softly.

'I was seven.'

'That's tough,' said Simi. 'I'm sorry to hear that.'

He shrugged. 'It's been a very long time now.' But Simi sensed his hurt.

'And you like the boarding school?' she asked quickly, to change the subject.

'It's OK,' he said. 'One of my aunts lives in Lagos, and I sometimes go to see her and my cousins at the weekend.'

'That's cool.'

He turned towards her. 'What about you? I still haven't really understood the reason for your visit. You said your parents sent you here because they did not have time for you?'

'They got divorced last year and my mum has to go abroad for work. And since I live with my mum and she was reluctant to send me to my dad and his new girlfriend, she preferred to send me here.'

'And you did not want to come here?'

She shrugged. 'Apart from the fact that I had never met my grandmother before now? Sorry, this may sound snobbish, but no electricity, no TV, no mobile phone network, no music, no running water? Sounds more like punishment than a holiday, don't you think?'

Jay laughed loudly. 'Yes, you're right. Poor ajebutter city kid.'

She playfully punched his arm.

'Ouch,' he said, laughing even more. 'But they do have music in Ajao. They have the best drummers. One of the families there even trains all the drummers in the area.'

'Really?'

He nodded. 'They are known far and wide, and people come from miles away to order their drums in Ajao.'

'Wow, that's amazing, though!' Simi said.

'Tonight's party is one of their famous drum festivals. We should get going. It'll soon be dark and the festival will begin.'

She groaned. 'It was so nice to chill up here.'

'Come on!' Jay cried, jumping up. 'The drums of Ajao are calling!'

14

The Ajao Drum Festival

From afar the village was brightly lit. A blurred orange cloud shrouded the village from the darkness of the surrounding night. Rhythmic drumming floated towards Jay and Simi as they ran along the path that led back to Ajao.

When they arrived, Simi saw a bright circle lighting up the large open space that served as the village centre, where the children had been playing football earlier. Hundreds of kerosene lamps had been placed around the space and dancing figures flitted around them like oversized termites. Ghostly smoke from a fire rose through trembling palm trees into the moonlit sky.

Simi felt excitement well up in her as she

133

watched the spectacle. A crowd of people had formed a circle and there was loud clapping and singing. Some older girls were dancing within the circle. They danced with so much fire that the dust whirled up and their headscarves flew off their heads. Next to them, a group, young and old, played different musical instruments. Simi recognized the hourglass shape of the 'talking' drums that some of the men clasped tightly under their arms, beating rhythms that told stories with curved sticks like umbrella handles. Bigger bata and gbedu drums were placed on the ground in front of some young men with bare torsos who beat the drums fiercely. The muscles on their arms were taut and their upper bodies glistened with sweat. A young man whose legs glinted with white efun patterns struck the metallic agogo with a short stick and danced and jumped around in a frenzy. Simi also saw several young girls hitting colourful shekeres against their palms. The shaker gourds covered with colourful beads made rustling rhythmic sounds to accompany the drums. Some other girls danced with agbalumo fruit kernels tied around their ankles. They jerked their feet to the rhythm, rustling the kernels and adding to the music. Another group of people sat a little further away and sang. The mood was fiery, and Simi stood there as if under a spell until she heard Jay call her.

'Hey, come on, city kid!'

As they pushed through the crowd, the heat of the people and the lanterns rushed through her bones in rhythmic waves, loosening her joints and muscles, making her want to dance.

She loved the traditional Yoruba dances and had been a member of the Yoruba cultural dance group in school. For two years she had danced and performed with the group until it had been classified as uncool by the older girls and most of them had moved to the hip-hop group. The Yoruba dance group had then been cancelled because it had lost too many members. Simi had been very disappointed, because she had loved the performances at the school events. But then she had switched to learning all kinds of African dances on the internet and had become really good.

A little girl appeared in front of them, shaking her waist and grinning cheekily.

'Bubu!' Simi cried, glad to see her.

She was wearing a red, flowery cloth, which was tied with a knot at the side of her chest and went down to her knees. Colourful beads adorned her neck, wrists and waist. Two agbalumo bracelets rattled at her ankles, which she moved expertly to the rhythm of the drums. She began to dance even more fiercely and Simi marvelled at her skilful moves. Bubu was amazing! Jay began to clap and cheer enthusiastically and Simi joined in.

A young woman approached with a smile. It was Kikelomo, the mother of the sick child she and Iyanla had visited two days ago. She was holding a large calabash with a long neck and held out two cups to them.

'If you want to dance, you have to drink zobo first,' Kikelomo shouted over the music as she poured red hibiscus juice into their calabashes.

'Is your son feeling better?' Simi asked.

'Thank you so much for asking. Yes, he is much better.' Kikelomo smiled brightly. 'Iyanla's medicine always helps us.'

Jay took the cups from Kikelomo and held one out to Simi.

'Ajao zobo is the best, because we always add lime and some other secret ingredients.' Kikelomo watched her sip.

'Oh, this is really good,' Simi replied and smiled at her. The taste was really pleasant and she realized she was quite thirsty after their walk under the hot sun. 'Thank you.'

Kikelomo balanced the calabash back on her head. 'You are welcome,' she said, and danced away.

'Come on, let's go watch the dancing,' Jay said, pushing through the crowd. Bubu had disappeared, so Simi followed him.

'Where are all the people from? There are no more than twenty houses in Ajao!' she shouted in his ear.

'I told you that the Ajao drum festivals are very popular. These are people from other villages.'

They joined the circle that enclosed four dancers, two young men and two women. The men tried to ensnare the women's attention and the women pretended to ignore them. It was like a kind of play. The women danced first while the men watched. Then the men had to dance and prove themselves worthy of attention by dancing well enough. And if the women found them worthy, only then would they turn around and let the men dance with them. Everyone clapped and cheered as other dancers went into the circle to have their turn.

Each dancer brought a new dance into the circle. Simi planned to practise some of them when she got back home. Although she felt a bit shy, she could not stop her hips and feet from moving. It was simply impossible to stand still with the music.

On the other side of the circle, she saw Iyanla's friend and Bubu's grandmother, Mama Ayoola.

'I should look for Iyanla and tell her I'm back,' she called to Jay.

'She's probably with the elders,' he replied.

But just at that moment someone blocked their way. It was Kikelomo again, balancing the calabash precariously on her head as she swayed her hips.

'You children still have to dance, oh. You can't leave yet,' she shouted and pointed to the circle.

The people around her opened the circle. Simi

shook her head in shock. Jay raised his hands in panic and tried to get them both out, but the circle was already cheering and they were pushed in.

Simi had the feeling that the music had suddenly become louder. Her heart thrashed in her chest, as if it wanted to keep up with the loud music. She looked at Jay, who smiled apologetically and also looked nervous. His uncertainty gave her courage; she took a deep breath and relaxed. She wasn't alone in this and, after all, she had often danced in front of the whole school when they presented their rehearsed choreographies on parents' day.

She summoned up her courage and spun around, circling her waist as she had seen the other women do. The crowd cheered and Jay's eyes widened in surprise. He spread his arms and slowly began to move his feet to the rhythm of the drums. The crowd cheered him as well. Probably no one had expected that they would really be able to dance. After all, she was a city granddaughter and Jay a city son, and neither of them were dressed in traditional clothes like the others. But Simi just held the hem of her oversize T-shirt as if it were a wrapper around her waist. She bent forward and fired her feet to the beat and the dust rose around her. She saw Jay grinning, and he bobbed his shoulders to the rhythm and then jumped in the air like Simi had seen the previous dancers do. When he landed, he began to tap his feet in one of the latest dance steps. He was actually a great dancer and knew how to move smoothly and gracefully.

'Wow, I never knew that Lagos girls could dance like that!' he called over the drum beats.

'Chief's sons that attend school in Lagos are not that bad either,' she replied, laughing.

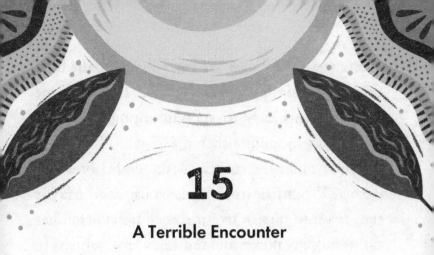

15

A Terrible Encounter

When they were too exhausted to dance any more, Simi and Jay left the cheering circle and went to look for Iyanla. They passed scattered groups, laughing, eating and talking loudly. Some people had taken out little three-legged ijokos and sat some distance from the music. Children ran giggling through the crowds, happy that they could stay up and play longer. A little further on, they found some elders sitting under a tree with a wide crown that, in the dark, looked like an oversized umbrella. This was the ube tree she was meant to find on her first day, Simi had since discovered. It was quieter here, but nevertheless there was a good view of the dancers and drummers. The elders sat on wooden chairs and, despite the darkness between the few kerosene lamps, it was easy to spot the upright, slender figure of her grandmother.

'But Iyanla, do you think the gods are angry with us?' Simi heard a male voice ask. 'Maybe they want to punish us for something. Oshun has taken more children and the rains have refused to come. My maize is ruined and Baba Femi's yams as well.'

'Ah, the young people have come to greet us,' said an elderly man with a grey beard, stopping Iyanla's reply.

'Ekaale, sir, Ekaale, ma.' Simi curtseyed, her knee touching the ground while Jay touched his fingertip to the floor and bowed his head.

'They have not forgotten us. It is well,' another man said. 'How is your father, Jide?'

'Thank you very much, sir. We thank God that he is fine.'

'And your aunts?'

'Thank you, sir.'

'And this is the granddaughter of Iyanla that has finally come home?'

'Be-eni, it is me, sir,' Simi replied shyly.

'What is your name, granddaughter of Iyanla?'

'Oluwanifesimi.'

'Very good, my child. And how is your mother?'

'Very good, thank you, sir.'

'I see you have been having a good time,' Iyanla cut in.

Simi smiled at her, wondering if Iyanla had deliberately come to her aid by preventing too many questions about her mum.

'Iyanla's granddaughter showed the girls here how they dance in Lagos,' Jay said.

The elders laughed. 'It is true. It is true,' they said, and everyone turned to look at her.

Simi felt shy and would have loved to shut Jay up.

'The city people are not as backward as one would think,' he added.

The elders laughed again.

'You really have the clever tongue of your father, my boy,' said one. 'You have to greet him from me. Tell him that Adesina of Iroola greets him. I went to school together with his father in those days, to learn the white man's language and his letters. A good man, your grandfather.'

'I will tell him, sir. Thank you very much.'

They were about to leave when the elders turned to look past them. Simi heard a squeaking noise. A man on a bicycle was slowly approaching. Just before he reached them, he stopped and dismounted. Simi recognized the man from the forest.

He stood in front of the group and for a brief moment it was as if he was unsure what to say.

'Ekaale, Baba Morayo,' someone called.

'It is not a good evening,' the man replied roughly.

The elders moved restlessly in their seats.

'What do you mean, Baba Morayo?' Iyanla asked sharply.

'Another child could go missing while you are all celebrating here,' came the brusque reply.

'Baba Morayo, we know things have been tough for you,' said Iyanla's friend, Mama Ayoola, who had just arrived.

Simi saw Bubu hiding behind Mama Ayoola and holding on to her elbow.

'My daughter was taken by that cursed lake of Oshun! It was not the time, but nobody cares!' Baba Morayo had raised his voice now and his whole body trembled with emotion.

Iyanla got up and Mama Ayoola placed a hand on her arm. The three other elders leant forward.

'But of course we care,' Iyanla said gently.

'So what is being done about it?' he cried. 'Your goddess is getting greedy! My Morayo should not have been taken! The goddess already has enough children. It was not time. Why did she take Morayo?'

Iyanla looked at him without fear, but sadness clung to her face.

'Why?' His voice was shrill.

Nobody spoke.

A cloud moved to cover the moon and it suddenly became darker and colder. A wind swished through the branches of the ube tree above their heads, and Simi began to shiver.

The man pointed a crooked finger, long and menacing, in Iyanla's direction. 'What do you have to say to that, Iyanla, priestess of the goddess Oshun?'

Iyanla stood her ground, her gaze unwavering.

'We do not know for sure that the children were taken by Oshun,' Mama Ayoola cut in quietly.

Baba Morayo let go of his bike and took a step forward. The bike fell to the ground with a clatter. 'We all know what has to be done! Each and every one of you knows that we have to close up that evil lake!'

The people around gasped. Mama Ayoola threw up her hands over her head.

Baba Morayo spat on the ground and the elders jumped up angrily, despite their old, rickety bones. Simi felt her palms become sweaty as she kneaded her fingers into each other.

'I think you should go home, Baba Morayo,' one of the men said in a tight voice. 'Because of what happened to Morayo, we will swallow your insults and look away. But you should definitely go now.'

But Baba Morayo did not even turn to look at him. His eyes remained fixed on Iyanla. 'Go to your goddess! Tell her enough is enough! Remind her of what was agreed. And warn her that we will fill in the lake!' He took a step towards Iyanla, towering over her.

'You of all people! You should know what it means to lose a child. I would have expected more support from you!' There were gasps at his words.

'Go home, Baba Morayo,' Iyanla said softly but firmly. 'We cannot fight a goddess.'

'Who says that?' he yelled. His whole body vibrated with tension. 'Who says that?'

Mama Ayoola hissed in shock.

'Do you know what?' he continued. 'I will tell her myself.' He hit his chest so hard it made a hollow sound. Simi jumped and Jay put a hand reassuringly on her shoulder. 'I will go to her right now. I know exactly where you always go. I know where her shrine is, back there where the river divides and passes close to the forest. I will call her there and scatter her shrine to pieces until she answers me and tells me where my daughter is.'

'No!' Mama Ayoola called. 'Baba Morayo, wait. That would be a desecration of the shrine. You cannot do that. Baba Morayo, think of the consequences for you and for all of us!'

'Why do you all still call me Baba of Morayo?'

His voice was a fierce, painful whisper, shredding the night. 'Do you see any child here named Morayo? I do not have a child any more. I do not have a name any more.' He turned abruptly, picked up his bicycle and left.

Mama Ayoola sighed. 'I will try to calm him down. Mama Morayo was my friend.'

Iyanla nodded, then she turned her back to everyone. 'Simi, let us go home,' was all she said.

16

Old Secrets

It was a huge relief to close the door behind them and block out the sound of the drumming and singing outside. The same rhythm that had fuelled her dance now pursued Simi like the tramping of furious spirits. She tried to think clearly.

Baba Morayo's words floated through her mind. She absolutely had to get Iyanla to tell her everything about the lake and the quicksands. Something about the story of Oya, Oshun and Layo had escaped her. But Iyanla had gone straight to her room without a word, and Simi did not dare go after her.

With trembling hands, Simi took her blanket

from the sofa bed in the living room and wrapped herself in it. Then she sat restlessly in the dark.

A gleam of light spilt through the crack beneath the bedroom door. She heard rustling noises, as if Iyanla was searching for something. Shortly after, the door opened and Iyanla stood there, holding a lantern.

She placed the lantern on the table and Simi saw that she was holding something in her hand. It looked like a piece of card.

'Did you eat anything at the festival?' Iyanla asked, peering at her.

Simi shook her head. 'I'm not hungry.'

Iyanla was still studying her. 'Do not worry about anything, Simi. All you have to do is keep away from the forest. Then you will be safe.'

Simi was definitely not planning to go anywhere near the forest. She tried not to think of what had happened to her at the lake, but goose-bumps covered her arms as she thought of the missing children.

'Iyanla, what did Baba Morayo mean? Why was his daughter taken by the lake?'

'I honestly do not understand it either,' Iyanla

said. 'As we were told, the lake of Oshun will call a child every ten years. But something has changed. What Baba Morayo said is true. Things are not like they used to be.'

'His heart is broken,' Simi said softly.

Iyanla nodded. 'His wife could not cope with the grief. She moved back to her people. He has not been the same ever since.' She suddenly looked extremely frail. She tucked the piece of card inside her wrapper. 'To lose a child is the greatest pain of all.'

'I do not understand. Why are you all still here?' Simi asked indignantly, suddenly feeling angry. 'If something terrible has been happening here for centuries, why does everyone not just move away?'

'You cannot run away from your fate. What is meant to happen, will happen.'

'But that is so . . . frustrating!' Simi cried.

Iyanla shrugged. 'We grew up here. The land belongs to us and we belong to the land. Before Morayo, the last child that was taken, just a few years ago, was a boy from another village. Nobody saw how he went to the lake. But Oshun called him. He belonged to her and we cannot fight her will.

'And many do not even feel threatened,' Iyanla went on. 'They no longer believe in the power of the gods and goddesses, and believe that the children drowned in the quicksands. As you heard yesterday, even the brother of the chief does not believe in the sacredness of the land any more. He is one of those who wants to sell the land and fill in the lake.'

'What if they do?' Simi almost feared to hear Iyanla's reply.

'If it is not her will, Oshun will not allow it.' Iyanla made a hissing sound. 'The decision will be made at the meeting in Ekita tomorrow evening. That is why I have to go to her shrine this night. I have to speak with her.'

Simi's eyes widened. 'You will talk to the goddess Oshun?'

Iyanla nodded, though she did not look certain. 'I just do not know if she will have an answer for me.'

'But Baba Morayo! He said he was going to scatter Oshun's shrine to pieces!'

'I do not think he would be that stupid. Mama Ayoola will calm him down. She knows him well.'

Iyanla gripped the handle of her door, but Simi still felt uneasy. There was something Iyanla had not yet told her.

'He was so angry with you,' she said to her grandmother. 'Why does he blame you so?'

Iyanla sighed. She sat next to Simi on the sofa bed and gently pulled out the piece of card from between the folds of her wrapper. Simi took it and held it towards the light of the lantern.

It was a photo of two children, old and faded, but Simi immediately recognized the red clay of Iyanla's house in the background. And she recognized the young girl. She was about the same age as Simi. She had a serious expression on her face and her eyes looked as if they wanted to dare the person behind the camera to do something. She wore a simple dark-green dress and she was barefoot.

'My mother!' Simi said softly, running her thumb over the picture. And while she did that, she looked more closely at the little boy beside her, whose hand her mother clutched tightly. He was maybe seven years old, wearing just shorts, with a big, dreamy smile and a distant look as he stared at the camera. He had put one foot on the other and placed one hand casually on his hip. Simi spotted that he was holding a little wooden toy car. And then suddenly it all became clear to her. The children looked very alike. Too alike to be just friends or cousins.

She drew in a sharp breath.

'Mum has a brother?' Simi asked. She stared at the photo again, trying to gather her thoughts into a straight line.

'She has a brother?' she repeated, a cold rage filling her stomach. All her life she had felt abnormal because she had not had a single relative in her life. 'Everyone has at least one relative!' her teacher had once said in front of the whole class, and the other kids had laughed. She had felt like an alien. And all this time, she had an uncle.

When Iyanla did not reply, she turned abruptly to her and froze. The old woman's eyes were blurred with tears.

'I am not surprised that she did not tell you

about Toyin,' Iyanla said. 'Since the day he left us, she has never once spoken his name.'

Simi's heart sank into her stomach. 'Where did he go?'

Iyanla took a deep breath. When she finally replied, her eyes were dry and distant.

'Toyin went to the forbidden lake in the forest. He went to Oshun's lake and he never came back.'

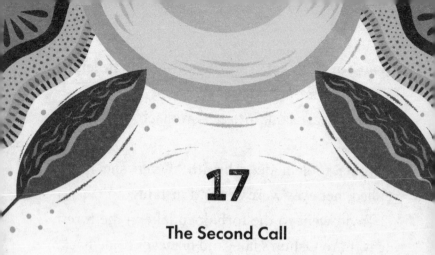

17

The Second Call

Simi woke up with a scream. She was drenched in sweat, her face was wet with tears and at first she did not know where she was. She was shaking all over, looking around frantically in the dark. Something had woken her. She had heard a call.

Confused, she tried to focus. Flashbacks of her dream raced through her mind. Quivering red sandhills and a strange purple sky. She had dreamt that she was beneath the lake. In the world below. She had seen her uncle Toyin there! She sat up with a pounding heart.

The delicate boy from the photo, shirtless, had been waiting for her at the lake. He had jumped up when he saw her and run towards her with outstretched arms and hopeful eyes.

'There is evil. There is fear,' he said.

'Why?' she had asked. 'Don't be afraid!' She had wanted to calm him, but didn't know how.

He shook his head. 'Help us.' His large eyes filled with tears and his lips began to tremble.

And that was when she had heard the call.

A sound like wind swishing over sand. A haunting birdsong. Telling her to come. Then she had woken up and found herself back in bed.

Simi closed her ears and forced herself to breathe more calmly. She was so hot. She pushed the sheet away and tried to calm down.

The moon threw a diagonal ray of white light through the little window. It was such a clear, strong light that she felt if she got up and reached for it, she would feel it between her fingers.

Suddenly she heard a sound from the direction of Iyanla's room. The creak of the door opening and a rustling. A shadow filled the doorway.

Simi held her breath as the slim figure of her grandmother moved silently across the room, cutting through the ray of moonlight. One half of

Iyanla's face was painted white and the other half was covered in white spots. She wore a white cloth around her body and she moved slowly, almost rhythmically. When she reached the passage to the backyard, she stood still for a brief moment. A low hum filled the room and Simi watched Iyanla move her bare left foot forward and then back beside the other. Iyanla did this movement three times and each time it was accompanied by the low rhythmic hum, as if she was praying. Then she opened the back door and disappeared into the night.

Simi must have fallen asleep again, but she had no idea for how long. She jerked out of it to find herself holding her pillow tightly.

She had heard the call again.

This time it crept through her ears into her entire body, making every nerve tingle. She got up. The house was silent.

She found herself moving along the corridor and out into the backyard. The cool night air brushed her arms and she shivered. She could distinctly hear the call, the strange melody of the golden bird. She raised her eyes in the direction of the forest and saw a bright flash in the distance between the treetops.

She wanted to run back into the house and cover her ears. But her feet began to move, one in front of the other, until she reached the little wooden gate.

She knew she should stop.

She reached out and pressed the latch. On the horizon she saw a bright streak. The sky was slowly clearing and the night would soon raise its dark cloak. In the distance, she heard the screams of monkeys and wondered if they sensed what was going on. She tightened her grip and pushed the gate open.

'What are you doing?' The voice of Iyanla cut sharply through the darkness.

Simi was so shocked that she found herself gasping. It took a moment before she recognized Iyanla, wading through the stream in her direction. She had a grim look on her painted face and was holding a calabash filled with water. Had she walked through the stream the whole way back from the shrine? Simi avoided her gaze and tried to gather her thoughts. What was she doing out here? Had she not seen something? Heard something? She looked in the direction of the forest. There was nothing to be seen. No golden bird. Had she only dreamt it?

'I . . . do not know,' she stuttered. 'I think I dreamt . . .'

Iyanla's eyes softened. She placed the calabash beside the path and waded out of the stream. The hem of her white wrapper was wet and dripped on to her bare feet as she led Simi back to the house and sat her on the sofa bed. She picked up the sheet and put it over Simi's trembling shoulders.

'Wait here. I will make you a herbal tea that will give you energy and warm you up. You're trembling all over.'

'Thank you,' Simi mumbled.

'If a person penetrates the world of spirits too deeply in their sleep,' Iyanla said, 'then it is difficult to find the way back into reality.'

Simi shuddered. Had she entered the world of spirits, or had the spirits come to her?

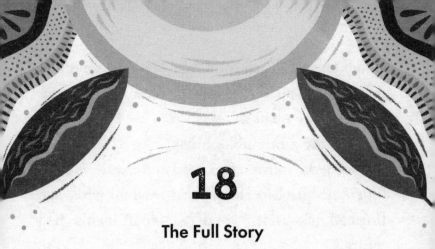

18

The Full Story

Later that morning, Simi woke up thinking of her mum. The events of the night seemed so strange and obscure in her memory, and the only thing she could think of was how poor Mum had lost her little brother in the lake.

The sun was already high in the sky. Simi glanced at her watch and saw it was almost ten o'clock. She jumped up, grabbed her toothbrush and toothpaste, and went out to the backyard. The air outside was thick and the sun crashed its heat down on her so heavily it almost made her gasp.

A shadow passed over her head and Simi looked up to see dense dark clouds overhead. But almost immediately their colour diluted, the clouds changed their forms and were driven off by the winds. The sky seemed to be in motion, not able to make up its mind.

'Even the air trembles today.'

Simi jerked around to see Iyanla watering the little herb garden. She greeted her and while she brushed her teeth wondered what Iyanla had meant.

Iyanla was quiet and tense this morning. From time to time Simi caught her staring into space with an absent look. Sometimes she would mumble to herself.

Simi kept herself busy. She swept the whole yard and the house. She helped Iyanla cook and prepare her salves.

'Will you still go to Ekita today?' Simi asked over lunch. They were having yam and bitter-leaf stew and Simi realized how hungry she was after skipping dinner the night before. Iyanla had hardly eaten anything.

'Both of us will go,' Iyanla answered.

'Didn't you say you always leave very early to avoid the afternoon heat?'

'The chief will send someone for me.'

'Did you get an answer yesterday night?'

Iyanla shook her head wearily. 'The goddess is in a very bad mood. I can feel it in the air and in her waters. She did not reply. Something is definitely wrong.' Iyanla dropped her fork. 'I do not want you wandering around alone any more. You should be careful. We do not know what is going on and I cannot . . . your mother cannot lose you too.'

Simi swallowed nervously. Iyanla was obviously referring to her sleep-walking the night before.

'It is because of Toyin that Mum does not speak to you, right?'

Iyanla nodded.

'Does she . . . does she think . . .' Simi wasn't sure how to ask her question without hurting Iyanla, but her grandmother cut her short.

'Yes, she blames me for it. Although I think, deep down, unfortunately, she blames herself too.'

'But that's unfair to you and to her!' Simi cried. 'It is not either of your faults!'

Iyanla stared at her for a while before replying. 'Toyin was born with a restless heart,' she said. 'Only one half of it was in this world. He loved the stories about the gods and goddesses. He would sit outside under the moonlight on a straw mat in the backyard every night, waiting to hear the stories. He was always the first of the children to be there, and would call the other children from the neighbourhood to hurry up. But it was the story of Layo he loved the most. He would not give me any rest until I had told it.'

She took a deep breath before continuing.

'It is not as if the other children did not also love the stories. But Toyin was not content just to hear the stories. He wanted to experience them. To live them. He began inventing stories about Layo's world.'

Iyanla sat rigid, staring at her uneaten plate of yam.

'Your mother was the exact opposite,' she went on. 'She ridiculed the stories. She did not believe them. To this day, she believes that all the children who disappeared just drowned.' Iyanla's gaze turned hard. 'But he is not dead,' she said a little louder. 'I know, even if he is gone, that he is not dead. He is with Layo.'

Simi realized that her grandmother wanted this

to be the truth. Desperately! Simi wanted to put an arm around her shoulders and comfort her. But she sensed it was not something Iyanla would approve of. So she kept her arm to herself.

'How old were they when it happened?' she asked instead.

'Your mother had just turned seventeen and Toyin was eleven years old. There was a very special bond between them. She was always very protective of him. And the day it happened . . .'

Iyanla broke off and took a deep breath. 'It was a day I had gone to the market in Ekita. That day, as far as I understood from what I was told afterwards, they had had an argument. It was the year when another child was to go and join Layo. But the year was almost over and Biola had told Toyin that the stories were all nonsense and that no child was going to go anywhere. She told him to forget his stupid fantasies. And he got very angry. She had underestimated how important it all was to him. He jumped up and said he would prove it to her, so that she would finally believe.

'He ran off and she immediately guessed what he wanted to do. She ran after him, but he was too fast for her. They ran through the forest, all the way to the forbidden lake. Your mother pleaded and called after him, begging him to turn back. But she arrived at the lake only to watch him jump in.'

Simi was speechless. She stared at Iyanla, whose eyes were brimming with tears.

'Your mother was not afraid of anything,' Iyanla said.

Simi tried to imagine this totally different version of her mother: one who was not afraid. She could not. She only knew her mother as someone who worried about everything and who was afraid of everything.

'They told me she jumped in after him. Again and again she dived into the lake searching for him. A woman from the village had seen them running into the forest. She collected several neighbours and they went after them. It took ten people to pull Biola out of that lake. Otherwise she would not have stopped.'

Iyanla sighed. A deep, painful sigh that brought tears to Simi's eyes.

'She never spoke to me again. Soon after that she finished school and left Ajao, and I have not seen her since. And I cannot even blame her. A person is not firewood. There is a limit to what a person's body can take.'

Iyanla looked tiredly at Simi. 'Both my children were taken from me that day,' she said quietly. 'That is how the gods are. They scatter fates like a farmer throws out seeds on his land. Some people's fates are fertile, easy-to-cultivate seeds that grow into strong plants and bear fruit. While the fates of some others are hard, empty husks that wither and die.'

Simi did not know what to say. She was too shocked by all she had just heard. She now understood her mother's constant panic that something could happen to her. She also finally understood her fear of water. If Simi so much as stepped in a puddle, her mother would begin to worry. She had never been allowed to go swimming, or to any beach parties. Her mum had made sure she'd had swimming lessons when she was eight years old. She had sat beside the pool like a soldier, watching Simi's every move and watching the swimming instructor like a hawk. And after that she had never let Simi go near water again.

Simi felt awful for her mum and cursed this village where she could not even make a phone call. More than anything now, she would have loved to call her mother to reassure her that she was fine, to console her. But then she remembered that her mum was already in England on her training workshop. She felt very far away and helpless. Her longing for her mum was so strong that it hurt.

'Try not to worry, my child.' Iyanla seemed to sense her sadness. 'Just don't go out alone for now until we find out what is happening.'

Simi nodded. She was definitely going to keep safe.

'Eavesdropping is a bad habit,' Iyanla suddenly said, raising her voice.

'Heh?' Simi said, confused.

Iyanla turned her head. 'If you keep eavesdropping, you might one day hear things that will make your ears rot and fall off.'

Simi heard a rustling in the bushes outside the gate, and the upright plaits of Bubu appeared between the leaves.

'I did not hear anything,' she whispered, looking worried and holding her ears.

19

Thick Air and Splashing Streams

'Sit down with us, like a sensible child,' Iyanla said, without turning around. 'Are you hungry?'

Bubu did not need more than one invitation. She came up to Iyanla and greeted her with a curtsey. Then she washed her hands in the bowl, and sat next to Simi.

When she saw Iyanla looking at her expectantly, Simi jumped up and prepared a plate of yam and bitter-leaf stew for their guest.

'Where are your sandals, Bubu? Are you not too old to run around barefoot?'

Bubu shook her head in her usual stubborn way. Obviously she had more to say, and nodding or shaking her head was not going to work. She finally made a decision to speak. 'I forgot my slippers outside yesterday night and when I woke up this morning, they were arranged in a criss-cross in front of my bed.' She looked at Iyanla meaningfully.

'And so they will never ever be worn again? Don't tell me the bushbabies have left their business of crying in the forest and nowadays arrange slippers in front of beds?' Iyanla asked.

Simi chuckled as she placed the plate in front of Bubu. Her grandmother kept a straight face while Bubu looked at her in shock.

'No. Not the bushbabies! It was the spirits of the night! The Egun!' She was whispering again. 'They want me to dance to their music.' She looked around fearfully. 'If I put my feet in those slippers, I will be forced to dance to their music and will never *ever* be able to stop dancing!'

'Did you even bother to ask your grandmother if she placed the slippers in front of your bed?'

Bubu looked at Iyanla sharply, her eyes slanting in realization. Then she grinned sheepishly.

'I thought as much.' Iyanla shook her head.

'Bubu, how many times has your grandmother told you to stop these silly thoughts? Not everything that happens is juju.'

Bubu nodded her head vigorously, her eyes on the plate.

'OK, eat your food now!' Iyanla said with a shake of her head. 'Then you can show Simi how to wash clothes at the stream, since it doesn't look like you are very busy.'

Simi grabbed her dirty clothes and threw them into a metal bucket in which Iyanla had placed a piece of black camwood soap. Then she and Bubu walked along the little stream behind Iyanla's gate in the direction of the village. When they reached a spot where the stream widened, Bubu stopped and scrambled down the rocks to the water.

'Is it deep?' Simi called.

Bubu shook her head. 'It hasn't rained in weeks. The stream is almost dry.' Simi filled the bucket by holding it against the thin stream of water. She got it half full with surprisingly clean water and brought it back up. She began scrubbing the clothes but the heat was unbearable and she was soon soaked in sweat. Bubu, who had been wading through the stream, came to help her scrub the red dust out of her dresses. She shook her head at what Simi was doing and showed her how to hold the dirty spots and scrub properly.

'Thanks,' Simi mumbled.

They washed and scrubbed in companionable silence until Bubu tapped her arm with a soapy finger.

Simi looked up, but Bubu just stared at her and swallowed without speaking.

'Yes, Bubu?'

Bubu cleared her throat and slanted her head in a nod towards the stream. 'She is not going to allow it.'

'Who? What?'

'She is not going to allow them to fill in the lake.' Bubu bobbed her head towards the stream again and Simi realized she meant the water goddess, Oshun.

'That's what Iyanla said too.'

'She can be quite cunning.'

'Iyanla?'

'No, I mean *her*!' Bubu rolled her eyes and bobbed her head towards the stream again.

'Why do you say so?'

'Well, you know the story of how when she was married to the god Sango, she tricked his second wife into cutting off her ear and putting it into his soup to make him love her more!'

'What?' Simi laughed at the strange story, not believing a word.

Bubu sighed. A deep, desperate sigh. 'I am being serious.'

'I am sorry,' Simi said, 'but it's a weird story.'

Bubu frowned, looking offended. 'Since then she and the second wife hate each other. Whoever is travelling on the river of the goddess Oshun never mentions the name of the other wife because their boat could sink.'

'And what's the other wife's name?' Simi asked.

'Her name is—' Bubu replied, but then realized what she was about to do and clamped her hand across her mouth.

At the same moment the stream made a sudden swishing sound. Water gurgled up and splashed out, hitting them.

Bubu yelped. In two great leaps she was up the rocks. She drew a circle in the air above her head and snapped her fingers to fend off evil. 'God forbid bad thing,' she muttered.

'Relax, Bubu, it's just a stream,' Simi said.

But the stream gurgled even more loudly as she said it.

They grabbed the clothes and the bucket, and ran off screaming.

Iyanla did not ask why they were back in such a hurry, or why Simi finished the washing with water from the well. And Bubu had decided to stop talking for the rest of the day.

When they heard a knock on the front door, Iyanla shook her head. 'That is Jide,' she said. 'Only city people knock on an open door and then wait for someone to come and take them by the hand and lead them inside.'

Simi grinned. 'It's open,' she called. 'We're in the backyard.'

Jide appeared in the doorway. 'Ekaason, ma. How is your body today, Iyanla?'

'Thank you, my boy, it is well,' she answered.

'How is your family?'

'Very good, thank you. Moktar and I were sent to pick you and Simi up for the meeting of the elders.'

Bubu slipped a cold, trembling hand into Simi's.

Simi smiled at her. 'Everything will be fine, Bubu. Don't worry, the elders know what they are doing.'

Iyanla raised an eyebrow as if to say she wasn't at all sure about that.

'I'll leave my Walkman here for you, OK?' Simi added. 'You can listen to it when I'm gone.'

Bubu immediately held out her hand.

The journey to Ekita felt as if they were driving through heat waves, each hotter than the last. It was as if there was a magnetic layer over Simi's skin. She watched beads of sweat gather on Moktar's forehead, just below his turban. The air con couldn't overcome the heat, so he turned it off and opened the windows. He seemed nervous, and every time he drove through a pothole he would glance at Iyanla, who was sitting beside him, as if worried that he wasn't driving carefully enough.

Iyanla was quiet and her mood had settled over the car. She had changed into a fine dark-blue aso-oke ensemble of blouse, wrapper and headscarf, woven with delicate golden threads. She looked impressive and a thick necklace of large traditional coral beads underlined her age and status.

Jay glanced at Simi. 'Do you also feel the air is strange today?' he whispered.

Simi nodded.

'It is Oya.' Iyanla spoke in a low, rhythmic voice, almost like she was reciting a chant. 'The air has been charged for days now. The rains are taking too long to come. The sky rumbles at night, ready to burst, but cannot release the rains. An angry wind keeps blowing the clouds away. I can feel Oya's presence. The air is full of her. It is stretched taut like goatskin around the mouth of a new drum.'

Simi shivered, even though the heat was almost unbearable. She pushed some stray braids back into her bun as the air crackled and hissed. She glanced at Jay uneasily before asking Iyanla, 'But why is she angry?'

'I do not know, my child. But there is definitely something going on up there. She is calling out to her sister Oshun. Oshun has not yet answered, but when she does, it will be a bigger storm than we have had for a long time.'

Simi looked into the sky, which was an unstable mix of blue, white and bursts of grey. 'Do you think her anger is related to the lake?'

'Everything is somehow related to everything,' Iyanla replied. 'I am afraid of Oshun's reply to her sister. If it is an angry one, then you do not want to be anywhere near her.'

'Why not?' Simi whispered fearfully.

'Because she will burst the clouds and break the banks of her rivers and pour the waters over the land,' Jay said softly.

'Yes. We have to be on guard,' Iyanla said.

Goosebumps crawled over Simi's back as she looked up at the restless sky. Dense dark clouds formed but were immediately driven off by the angry winds. A wave of stifling, humid air swirled around them like an invisible wet curtain, and then lightning struck. Two fat grey clouds smashed together and thunder exploded.

The silence after that was heavy.

When Iyanla spoke, her voice sounded dry and cracked as firewood: 'It has begun.'

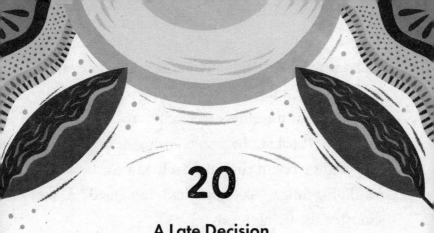

20

A Late Decision

Simi stared fearfully out of the window of Jay's living room.

A dry storm was raging. Lightning split the sky with sharp sparks of light, followed by ear-bursting thunderbolts. The air was charged, heavy and crackling. The clouds hurtled across the sky in a frenzy. But still no rain.

The meeting of the elders had lasted so many hours that Simi was beginning to get worried. She and Jay had talked about everything possible. Music was playing in the background, and scattered on the table before them were the remains of their dinner of jollof rice and fried plantain. Jay lay on a sofa, twisting a small football back and forth in his hands and occasionally bouncing it against the wall. At first, they'd gone to the main house every hour to see if the elders were close to an end. But each time Moktar had shaken his head. Finally, they had given up running back and forth underneath the angry sky and had remained in the safety of the living room.

In hushed tones they kept returning to the subject of the lake.

'I feel really bad for Morayo's dad,' Simi said.

'Losing someone close to you is not easy to get over. Such things take time.' Jay shook his head slowly and turned away, though Simi briefly saw hurt in his eyes. Simi realized he must be thinking of his mum.

'But it helps to know they are only somewhere else and that they have not stopped existing,' he continued.

'You mean, like, in heaven?'

'Yes – in Morayo's case maybe it will help her dad heal faster knowing that she is just somewhere else and not actually dead.'

'So you do believe the legend is true, then?'

'I really am not sure. It seems like a superstitious

story that grannies tell their grandchildren on moonlit nights. But if you've grown up here and you've seen strange things happen, then it does make you wonder. Ajao and the forests and villages around it have always been magical. They say the people and the land are one. Nature is rooted in the people, and that is why they see, hear and feel more than people elsewhere. That is why the power of the goddesses is still strong here.'

Jay shrugged. 'It's really weird, but anytime I come back from Lagos I feel the magic fizzing back into my blood. It is difficult to explain.'

'I think I know what you mean,' Simi replied. Since she'd arrived here, her whole world as she knew it had been turned upside down and things she would never have thought possible seemed absolutely normal.

'It would definitely be strange to lose the magic of the lake if it were gone,' Jay said. 'Everyone here grows up knowing about Layo and the goddess Oshun. If the lake is filled in, that which made our land so special will be gone for ever.'

Simi nodded and frowned as a thought crossed her mind. 'If it is filled in, the last connection to the world down there will be cut off. If there are children, they will never find their way back.'

Since Iyanla had showed her the photograph, she kept seeing the image of the little boy with the dreamy smile, holding his mother's hand.

Jay looked at her, surprised. 'No one has ever returned.'

'Yes, but . . . it could still happen someday,' she said weakly. What if she hadn't dreamt it? What if she had really been there? It had felt so real. And *she* had come back! What if there was a way . . .

'Are you thinking of your uncle?'

She nodded, overcome by sadness. She thought of her mother, and had to take a deep breath to steady herself.

'Should I get us some soft drinks?' Jay asked, sensing her mood and changing the topic.

A sudden loud knock made them jump. Jay went to the door, and Simi heard Moktar's deep voice.

'Mr Jide, Iyanla is ready to go. They are waiting for Miss Simi at the main house.'

'Yes, of course. I will bring her there,' Jay replied.

Simi ran to the door. But when she got there, Jay had already asked the question: 'Has the decision been made?'

Moktar nodded gravely.

'And?' Jay asked in an urgent tone.

Moktar looked uncomfortable, as if he did not want to reply. But then he said, 'The whole household is already talking about it, anyway.' He glanced at Simi. 'They will fill in the lake.'

Iyanla did not say one word on the way back home. The chief had taken the car keys from Moktar and said he would drive them to Ajao himself. Jay had also hopped into the car. Once in a while Simi and Jay glanced nervously at each other, but they did not dare say a word. Simi stared out of the window at the dark sky that constantly lit up like a firework. She felt numb with worry.

When they arrived in Ajao, it was immediately obvious that something was wrong. The whole village was dark, but in the compound beside Iyanla's house there were too many lights. It was Mama Ayoola's house. Immediately the chief parked the car, Simi heard someone shout, 'Iyanla is back!'

A dark shadow ran towards the car. 'Iyanla, please come!'

'What is it?' Iyanla asked quietly.

'Something terrible has happened!' It was only now that Simi recognized Kikelomo. She had her son tied to her back and her eyes were wide with worry. 'It is Bubu!'

Simi gasped and jumped out of the car, Jay behind her. She ran across Iyanla's front yard and through the hibiscus plants to Mama Ayoola's compound. Although it was almost midnight, the air was still hot and thick. The moment she left the chief's air-conditioned car, drops of perspiration formed on her temples.

Agitated voices came from Mama Ayoola's house, which was brightly lit by the swaying lanterns of the many people inside. Simi peered in through the open door. The tiny living room was brimming with people and they were speaking in anxious voices. Simi recognized most of them, and was surprised to see even Baba Morayo sitting on a chair in a corner, his face knitted into a frown.

But she couldn't see Bubu anywhere.

A terrible thought came to her. Had she been swallowed by the lake like Morayo? A door to a back room opened and Mama Ayoola came out. She was crying.

'Where is Bubu?' Simi cried.

'What happened?' Simi heard Iyanla's voice behind them.

'She is here. Come and see for yourself,' Mama Ayoola said.

Simi let out a sigh of relief, though she was still terribly worried. At least Bubu was here! Iyanla and the chief walked through and people made way for them. Simi followed, Jay too.

The room was dark and only lit by a candle. Bubu lay on a little mat on the ground.

Her eyes were wide open and she was staring at the ceiling. She looked confused.

Simi went closer. 'Bubu, what's wrong?' she whispered.

But Bubu did not respond. Though her eyes were wide open, they were not focused. Her pupils buzzed around nervously in her eye sockets.

Iyanla knelt down beside Simi and took Bubu's

hand. Then she placed her other hand on Bubu's forehead. Bubu did not react and didn't seem to notice their presence. A croaking noise came from her throat. It was as if she was trying to speak, but could not get the words out.

Simi glanced at Iyanla anxiously. 'What is wrong with her?'

Iyanla inspected Bubu's arms and legs and the back of her head. 'I cannot see anything physically wrong with her. What exactly happened?' she asked.

'It was Baba Morayo who found her,' Mama Ayoola said. She was leaning against the door frame and her voice sounded strange and came in jerks. 'She was in the forest, at the forbidden lake!'

'What? At Oshun's lake?' The chief spoke for the first time, and Mama Ayoola looked at him as if she was noticing him for the first time.

Simi glanced at Jay and saw that he looked just as shocked and scared as she felt.

Tears began to roll down Mama Ayoola's cheeks. 'What will I tell her parents?' she whispered. Kikelomo appeared at her side and led her away.

Iyanla took one last look at Bubu and then got

up. 'I must speak to Baba Morayo,' she muttered, and left the room. Simi followed her.

'Why has Oshun done this to my granddaughter?' Mama Ayoola asked. She was sitting beside Baba Morayo, her arms folded across her chest. Her eyes still glistened with tears, but they were hard and cold as she challenged Iyanla.

Iyanla shook her head. 'This has nothing to do with Oshun. It is as if Bubu is possessed. I have never seen anything like it, but I know that this is not Oshun's doing.'

She turned to Baba Morayo. 'What exactly happened?'

Baba Morayo had his fists clenched together on his thighs. He let out a tired sigh. 'I was in the forest, close to the forbidden lake, when I saw Bubu. She was heading straight there and I knew something was wrong. So I ran after her, calling her name. But she did not reply. She was almost in when I grabbed her and pulled her back. She looked at me, confused – she was in this state you've just seen her in. I sat her on my bicycle and pushed her through the forest back home. That is all.'

'Thank you so much, Baba Morayo,' Mama

Ayoola said with a shaky voice. She placed a hand on his arm. 'You saved my Bubu from that place!'

There were hushed whispers across the room and Simi noticed some people were staring at Baba Morayo with mistrust.

'Why were you there? What is your business at the lake?' an elderly man asked.

Simi couldn't help thinking about that first day she arrived in Ajao and how she had met him in the forest, on her way to the lake. How she had been scared of him, his sick-yellow eyes and ragged appearance.

Now Baba Morayo looked around the room with those same eyes. They were watery, hard and glaring. 'Since my one-and-only child was swallowed by that lake, I go to it every single day because that is where she is. What else should I do?' He clenched his fists again. 'That lake is an abomination and should long since have been filled in to protect our children.'

The chief cleared his throat. 'The lake is to be closed. The decision was made by the elders tonight,' he said.

'Finally!' Baba Morayo exclaimed.

There was an uncomfortable silence in the room as everyone realized what this could mean. Everyone glanced fearfully at Iyanla.

'What happened to Bubu is not Oshun's work. Filling in the lake is only going to cause more trouble.' Iyanla frowned. 'I need to consult the goddess again, but first of all I will prepare some medicine for Bubu . . . the root of ewúro, egbò ifòn and dried okofèe.' She shook her head. 'Fresh ata weere pupa, the bark of okìkàjà . . .'

Simi turned to Jay. 'I don't understand why Bubu would have gone there,' she whispered. 'She is so afraid of the forest, of the lake.'

But even as she spoke, Simi had a heavy feeling in her belly. A worrying thought that she tried to ignore but couldn't.

'When I pulled Bubu back from the lake,' Baba Morayo was muttering, 'she kept saying something about a bird.'

Simi stared at the old man. 'What kind of bird?' she heard herself asking out loud.

It was then that she realized: she knew exactly why Bubu had gone to Oshun's forbidden lake.

All eyes in the room turned to her.

21

Simi Confesses

'I... erm...' Simi felt like she was suffocating. Everyone was staring at her and she realized too late that she now had to say what had happened to her.

'Well, on the day of my arrival, I thought I saw a golden bird,' she said hesitantly, her eyes lowered. Iyanla had come to stand beside the chief, and Simi somehow could not meet her eyes.

'The bird hypnotized me with its song and sort of lured me to follow it. I'd never heard anything like it before. It is hard to describe. It was magical, beautiful, but almost too beautiful, like when you eat too many over-ripe mangoes and feel sick afterwards. I could not escape, I could not turn back. My legs followed the bird of their own accord.'

She paused and looked around. There was a dead silence in the room.

'Followed him where?' Iyanla asked.

'The bird took me to the forbidden lake,' she whispered.

A loud murmur went through the room and people edged closer.

Simi took a deep breath, her heart racing so fast she could barely squeeze out any more words. She felt a reassuring hand on hers and she looked up. It was Jay. He nodded encouragingly, but she could also see the surprise and confusion in his eyes.

'All this while,' Simi went on, 'I wasn't sure it was real, because it all seemed so strange, like I dreamt it. But . . . I saw that bird and it lured me down there,' she said finally, in a clear, determined voice.

Simi was sure everyone could hear her heart beating.

'What do you mean, "down there"?' Iyanla asked.

'To the world under the lake. I . . . I saw it, the

world that the goddess Oshun created for Layo. I was there!' Simi finished strongly. It was almost a relief to finally speak about what had happened to her.

Now the whole room went into a turmoil. Several people ran out screaming and others took careful steps towards the door, staring at Simi as if she were possessed. But the worst thing was the look on Iyanla's face. It was pain, mixed with a raw, naked fear.

'Iyanla,' whispered Simi. 'I'm sorry. I did not know . . . I thought I had only dreamt it, but when Baba Morayo mentioned the bird, I realized it must have been real . . .'

Iyanla suddenly swayed and the chief reached out to steady her. Jay grabbed the nearest chair. Iyanla, who was now terribly pale, sat down like an old, frail woman.

Everyone began speaking at once.

'But it cannot be,' Kikelomo said.

'Nobody has ever returned from there!' cried a young man.

'Maybe it is because she is the priestess's grand-daughter?' someone else asked.

Mama Ayoola got up. 'Please, I think it is best if everybody leaves now.'

'Ahn, ahn, Mama Ayoola, this concerns everyone,' Baba Morayo said.

But the old lady was firm. 'I will inform everyone of any new developments tomorrow morning,' was all she would say.

When everyone had left and the house was calm, the chief grabbed a chair and sat down beside Iyanla. Jay did the same. Mama Ayoola stood behind them and all four of them stared at Simi in disbelief.

Jay was the first to speak. 'Are you sure?' He swallowed nervously. 'I mean, maybe you really just imagined it?'

Simi looked at him. 'I did not want to believe it myself, and since the day it happened I have pushed the memory aside because it seemed so strange. But I did not even know the story of Layo then – Iyanla told me afterwards. And down there was the first time I heard the name Layo mentioned.'

'You mean there were people?' Iyanla interrupted. She sat upright, her arms taut at her side, her hands gripping the chair. Her eyes looked so hopeful that Simi immediately knew what she was getting at.

'Yes,' she replied gently. 'But I did not see Toyin.'

Iyanla looked away quickly and her eyes were expressionless again.

'But there are children there! I saw them clearly,' Simi said hastily. She told them everything about the world – the trembling hills, and the dark purple sky.

When she finished, everyone was silent again.

'But you did not react like Bubu,' Iyanla said.

Simi shook her head slowly. 'You saw me afterwards, Iyanla. I was only a bit confused.'

All of a sudden she had the most horrible thought. 'Oh, no! If I had said something earlier, then this would not have happened to Bubu!' She looked at everyone helplessly. Tears blurred her eyes and she buried her face in her hands. Jay was at her side immediately, and she felt his hand on her shoulder.

'Everyone here is as confused as you, my child,' Mama Ayoola said gently. 'No one knows what to think. And with these kinds of things, if they are meant to happen, they will happen. If there is an evil power behind all this, the power will find one way or another to get what it wants.'

Iyanla got up. 'Chief, I need a driver,' she said firmly. 'Simi has to go back home. To Lagos.'

Simi drew in a sharp breath. 'What?'

'I need a driver to take her home immediately,' Iyanla repeated.

'Iyanla, no! I cannot go home now. I don't want to leave Bubu like this! And besides, nobody is home.'

Iyanla ignored her and continued speaking. 'She is in the gravest danger. I know that it is asking a lot, especially under the circumstances. You may need your driver yourself.'

The chief raised his hands. 'Do not worry. Jay will also be leaving for Lagos. He will accompany her.'

'What?' Jay cried. 'Dad, I just arrived! I am on holiday!'

The chief turned to his son. 'I would feel much better knowing you are safe in Lagos at the moment. We can only hope that this . . . power does not reach as far as Lagos. I will also have the lake guarded.'

'But, Dad, I can help you with all these plans! I do not want to leave you now!'

His father raised a hand to stop him. 'I want to know that you are safe. I will send your little sisters to their mothers' home towns as well,' he said. 'That is the best support you can give me.'

Simi did not want to go back. Of course she was scared, yet she did not want to leave. First of all, she would have to go to her dad's. And she definitely had no desire to see him with his new girlfriend right now. And secondly, she had a strange, overpowering feeling that she was here in Ajao for a reason. She felt she had a role to play in this story, even if her role was only to help her grandmother.

As they walked to Iyanla's house, they saw people whispering in groups, who hushed each other and quickly turned away as they passed. Simi lowered her eyes and hurried after Iyanla.

Suddenly a huge flash of lightning struck across the sky and tore it in two parts. The people jumped and shrieked in fear.

Simi stared at the sky, waiting for the rumbling thunder. It came soon after, ear-deafening, crackling and vicious. The sky darkened. It was like a power cut: one moment it was bright and the next it was pitch black and people were running into their houses. Some of them drew crosses on their forehead and chest while scurrying away. The chief and Jay waved goodbye, jumped into the car and drove off.

Simi also wanted to run into the house, but she almost stumbled into Iyanla, who stood in her path, looking up. Another flash of lightning and another ripped the dark sky apart. The lightning bolts came so fast that the matching thunderclaps collapsed into one another to make such a deafening roar that Simi held her arms up to protect her ears.

Then lightning seemed to reach down all around them to hit the earth. One bolt hit the stream behind Iyanla's house and light exploded out of the water, illuminating the sky with a strange blue.

'There she is!' Iyanla said, as they hurried into the house. 'Oshun has finally shown her face.'

And then the rains came down.

22

Back to Lagos

Simi had only slept a few hours when Moktar and Jay arrived in the dark morning hours to drive her back to Lagos. Simi yanked on her clothes, feeling sad and frustrated. Iyanla held her tight for a brief moment and then she hurried to the car through the lashing rain. It poured down in waves as if it wanted to make up for all the missing weeks of rain in a few hours. Moktar drove at a tortoise pace, because it was almost impossible to see anything of the flooded road ahead.

But as soon as they had left the region, after an hour of driving, the rain stopped so abruptly that the silence was almost hurtful. The sky cleared and the pale light of dawn began to show itself.

The few villages they drove through seemed absolutely untouched and oblivious to the storm that raged only kilometres away. The air lost its charged feel and it was as if a burden had fallen off Simi's shoulders.

'Do you feel the strange difference?' she whispered.

Jay nodded. 'I feel like we just switched planets.'

Goosebumps crept over her back. 'It's scary.'

'But I hate that I have to leave now,' he added.

Simi felt the same way. She couldn't stop thinking about the little boy in the old photograph. Toyin: her uncle. And how sad her mother must have been all her life, never to have mentioned him. She cleared her throat and for the first time tried to speak about her own worries.

'When I was beneath the lake . . .' she said, trying to put her thoughts into words. 'It is difficult to explain, but somehow I had the feeling that the children were afraid.'

Jay raised an eyebrow. 'How do you mean?'

'It was the way they spoke, when they called the name Layo. So hushed. Anxious, fearful almost. It didn't sound like he was a playmate, as

Oshun intended. He sounded like someone they were scared of.'

'Why, what did they say?'

Simi tried to remember the words of the children. 'They just sounded afraid that Layo would be angry.'

She saw that Moktar was watching her in the rear-view mirror, and lowered her voice. 'I keep picturing my uncle in that place. But he may not even be alive any more.' Tears welled up in her eyes and she quickly turned to look out of the window. 'He has been missing for so many years, but I always have this picture Iyanla showed me in my mind. A little dreamy boy, who my mum absolutely wanted to protect. But could not. And I cannot help him either. I feel guilty, because for some reason I succeeded in going there and coming back. But he and so many others didn't. And now Bubu . . .' Her voice broke.

Jay patted her hand and she was grateful. They didn't speak much for the rest of the way.

To Simi's disappointment, it was Imona, her father's girlfriend, who opened the door of their

200

new house. Her father was at work. Simi had called him from Jay's phone as soon as they had signal. Her phone battery was dead. But her dad had not sounded very enthusiastic. He said several times that he would of course be happy to see her, but that it was bad timing and that he could not take any days off work at the moment.

'Daddy, I'm not a baby. I can stay alone during the day. It's not a problem.'

'Yes, but the holidays have just begun. Your mother had her good reasons for not wanting to leave you alone every day for weeks.' He'd sighed. 'Why couldn't you stay there – did you behave badly, or what?'

'Iyanla thought I was in danger,' she'd replied. 'Some children have disappeared and there is a goddess and a bird that lures—'

Her father had groaned loudly. 'Oh, please, not those stories! That's why your mother left Ajao, years back. She couldn't stand talk about juju and goddesses any more.'

After a brief silence, he'd said, 'OK, fine. Just come and we'll see when you get here. I'll think of something.'

Now Simi stood at the door and Imona was smiling at her much too brightly. She was wearing too much make-up. 'Please, do come in,' she said eagerly.

'Thank you,' Simi replied, stepping past her. Moktar brought in her big suitcase.

'We have to go immediately because Moktar is really tired. Will you be OK?' Jay whispered.

Simi nodded and smiled a tired smile. She hugged him awkwardly under the slightly bemused eyes of Imona.

'I'll call you tomorrow,' Jay said, looking embarrassed, and he and Moktar disappeared.

Simi pulled her suitcase through the hallway.

'You can take it straight to your room,' Imona said. 'I'll show you.'

The elegant house her father had recently moved into with Imona would have impressed Simi if she had not felt so uncomfortable. Imona walked ahead of her with swaying hips, and Simi couldn't help smiling to herself. Her mother used to call Imona 'Miss Akoko-Edo', the place she came from.

'She probably took part in her village beauty pageant,' she said to Simi once, 'and I am sure she wears high heels in the house, even when she cooks. Although I do not know how she can cut onions with those artificial fingernails.'

Her mother had not been so far away from the truth, Simi thought, as she looked down at Imona's feet. Even though she wasn't wearing high heels, her black, lacquered ballerinas with a huge golden bow in front weren't the type she had seen anyone wear indoors before. She would still have to ask her dad how she should address his girlfriend. She could not call her by her first name; that would be rude. But 'Miss Okai' also sounded strange. Luckily they were not married, so at least she would be spared having to call her 'mum' or 'mummy'. She wouldn't have called her that anyway, even if they were married. No way! She would rather not speak to her at all than call her 'mum'. But she wasn't going to worry about it. She would leave that to her dad to decide.

Imona opened the door to the spare room and Simi sat down on the bed. 'I'm very tired,' was the only thing she managed to say, with a half-hearted apologetic smile. Imona nodded and left her alone.

Simi glanced around the room. A bed, a

bedside table and a wardrobe. A photograph of the Lagos Lagoon and curtains in navy blue. It looked like a hotel room – and she felt very much a guest in her own father's house. She sighed, plugged her phone in, quickly picked her playlist, put the volume on the loudest and threw herself back on the bed. She had left her headphones with the old portable CD player beside Bubu's bed. She prayed that Bubu would soon wake from her trance.

Strangely, even though she was lying on a much more comfy bed than Iyanla's sofa, in a room with air conditioning and phone signal, she was missing Ajao. She began to hum vigorously along to the song in an effort to fight the tears that now squeezed themselves through her eyelids.

When her dad finally came back from work, Simi was feeling a little better. She would somehow survive the weeks here, she told herself. After all, she had television, her phone, music and all the other comforts of modern technology to keep her company. Her father hugged her with a warm smile, and Simi was surprised by the emotions that instantly came over her. She clasped her arms around him and squeezed him so tightly that he looked at her closely with a surprised smile. Either she had missed him so much, or the events of the last few days had worried her more than she had thought.

'Hey, honey bear,' he said, grinning. 'Have you grown again?'

She rolled her eyes. He had been calling her 'honey bear' since she was a kid, because as a toddler she always wanted to eat only bread with honey.

'Oh, my goodness, Daddy, I am not a little kid any more.'

He grinned and was just about to say something when his phone rang. Simi let him go and felt disappointed. The eternal ringing of his phone had also been one of the issues between her parents. Her father had a busy and important job in a large oil company and he had always brought work and stress home with him.

Imona did not seem to mind. She smiled at him and helped him take off his suit jacket as he spoke into his phone. Then she gently pushed him on to the sofa and pulled off his shoes. He winked at her and Simi quickly looked away. This intimacy between her dad and Imona was too private and embarrassing for her.

She quickly left the living room and walked into the kitchen to get cutlery for the dining table. Dinner was fried baby potatoes with shrimp omelette. She smiled at Imona and told her it was delicious, even though she found it very bland after Iyanla's spicy cooking. Her father received two more calls during dinner and then he had to prepare a presentation, so Simi went back to her room. She had barely exchanged more than ten sentences with him.

The night was awful.

She could not sleep and tossed around in bed for hours.

She was almost asleep when she heard a flutter. A sound like wings. She stiffened, and the hairs at the back of her neck stood upright as she opened her eyes and searched the darkness of the room. High above, in the corner of the room, was a tiny bright glow, a golden light which dimmed and swooped and became the dark silhouette of a bird hovering in front of her. She wanted to scream or get up and run, but she was paralysed. The bird opened its sharp, curved beak and a terribly sweet song streamed from its throat. She covered her ears and closed her eyes but it made no difference. The sweetness of the bird's song crept into her ears, then into her veins and into every cell of her body. When the singing stopped, she opened her eyes and saw the bird fading into the darkness. Its claws were gripping something which looked strangely like . . . her headphones . . .

Simi sat upright in her bed, her heart pounding. She was bathed in sweat and her face was wet with salty tears. She hurriedly switched on the small lamp on the bedside table and checked the room. There was nothing. No bird. She had dreamt it, that was all.

She fell exhausted on to her pillow, but did not dare sleep. She grabbed a book from her bag and read until dawn. Only when the first rays of sunshine shone through her window did she put the book down and sleep.

The next day was better. Imona and her dad had

both gone to work, so Simi could relax alone. She tried to recall what Imona did for a living. She vaguely remembered her being an artist or a stylist or something.

She took her time in the bathroom, because she knew the day would be long enough. When she was showered and dressed, she left the house and walked up to the main street.

She was stunned at the amount of people rushing past her in all directions. People in suits hurried towards the skyline of tall office buildings ahead while others in groups looked like they were meeting up for an early lunch. The roads were jammed with honking cars, screeching motorbikes and buses bursting with passengers. Hawkers carrying large trays of cold drinks and snacks on their heads dodged through the traffic, selling their wares. Loud music played at every corner and the smell of smoke, perfumes and roasted corn filled the air.

What a different world this was from Ajao! How strange that people's lives could be so contrasting.

She hurried into a shopping centre as the heat of the day began to descend on the city. She browsed through the shops, had a cream croissant and even tried on a pair of trainers in the sports shop to while away the time.

On the way back, she picked up a loaf of her favourite soft agege bread and some freshly fried akara, which she had not eaten for a long time. Back at the house, she exchanged a few text messages with a friend but did not mention anything about Iyanla or her adventures at the lake. She knew that no one would believe her anyway.

Simi turned the pages of a book and two of Imona's magazines and tried to read. But after ten minutes she threw them on the bed and groaned. She was terribly worried about Bubu and what was happening in Ajao, and it was hard to distract herself. Her dream about the bird and the head-phones had scared her. Why had she dreamt such a strange thing? Iyanla would have gone to Oshun's shrine by now. What would she find out?

Every now and then Simi would feel she could hear the song of the bird. Then she would look around in relief when she realized that it was just her imagination. It was just the memory of the horrible dream, she would tell herself. But she made sure to close all the windows and switch on the air conditioning. The soft, even humming of the air con calmed her. She looked at her phone every few minutes, hoping Jay would call. She wanted to hear if there was any news from his dad. But she didn't want to seem too pushy. After all, they had arrived only yesterday.

By the time Jay finally called, in her despair and impatience she had vacuumed the whole house, dusted the shelves, which had not really needed cleaning, and made enough muffins for ten people.

She squeezed her phone with trembling hands and almost shouted into it with relief.

'Hi, city kid,' Jay said. 'How does it feel being back in Lagos?'

'Oh, good . . . erm, actually, no,' she added. 'To be honest, I'm terribly worried.'

'I know what you mean. Same here!' he replied, his voice now sounding less enthusiastic.

'How is Bubu?' Simi asked.

'She hasn't woken up. I am sorry, Simi, I know she is your friend,' he said softly. 'She has got worse since yesterday. My dad sent a doctor. He said there is nothing physically wrong with her.

All we can do is wait and pray she wakes up.'

'Simi? What happened? How come you have a signal – where are you?'

When Simi heard the panic in her mum's voice, she immediately regretted calling her.

'Mum, I am fine! Really! I am with Dad. But I had to come back to Lagos.'

'Why, what's wrong?'

'Children have been disappearing in Ajao and Iyanla felt it was better to send me back.'

There was silence at the other end of the line.

'Mum?'

'The lake story?'

'Yes.'

'Oh, goodness, are those villagers going hysterical about their goddesses again? I knew I shouldn't have sent you there.'

'Mum. A girl disappeared . . . And another little girl, Mama Ayoola's granddaughter, Bubu, has fallen under a kind of spell and now she is in a trance. She is my friend!' Simi's voice broke and she couldn't speak any more.

'Oh, Simi, please don't cry. I am so sorry about

your friend and that you had to go through all this. I shouldn't have sent you there! At least she had the sense to send you back home. Thank God. You know what, I will see if I can cut my workshop short. We just finished the first block this week. I can do the other blocks next year. I will manage somehow.'

'No, Mum, there is no need! I'm fine here. Really! Imona is quite nice, actually. I didn't mean to have you worried. I . . . I just missed you so badly today, that's why I called.'

'Oh, hon! I am so sorry!'

After the phone call Simi googled everything she could find about the different Yoruba gods and goddesses, and in particular Oshun and Oya. She plunged into the legends about ancient times when the gods still lived among the humans on earth. She had to keep herself busy.

The more she read about Oshun, the closer she felt to her. She was a powerful goddess who could be quite spirited, but she was also warm-hearted and fair. Simi couldn't believe that she would hurt families and keep the villagers in constant fear by taking their children. Something was wrong, it didn't make sense.

By the end of the day, Simi felt so wretched she was even glad when Imona came back. She almost hugged her.

'Nice necklace,' Imona said. 'The blue stone is lovely.'

'Oh, thanks. My grandmother gave it to me,' Simi replied, stroking the smooth, cool stone at the base of her neck and thinking of Iyanla. Funny how she hadn't even wanted to go to spend her holidays with her and now, after less than a week there, she had been angry to be sent home. Back in Lagos, she felt out of place, like a plant that had been uprooted and carelessly thrown on a heap.

'Did your dad call you yet?'

Simi shook her head.

Imona looked sympathetic. 'He had to fly to Port Harcourt today and will not be back for two days. He said he'll call you later.'

Simi was so disappointed she almost cried again. But she wasn't surprised. He was always spontaneously flying somewhere or getting back late or forgetting to tell her that he wouldn't be around. That was her dad.

23

A Drastic Plan

Simi woke the next morning to the doorbell ringing. She scrubbed her face in two seconds and ran to the door in her pyjamas.

Jay stood at the door, grinning, and she was so happy to see him she nearly hugged him.

After she had hurriedly brushed her teeth and dressed, she got them two Cokes out of the fridge and they made themselves comfortable in the living room in front of the TV.

'Wow, your place is really cool,' Jay said.

'Well, this is not my place, to be honest,' Simi said. 'It's the house of my father and his girlfriend and I just have a guest room here.'

Jay said nothing but looked at her with a

raised eyebrow.

She shrugged. 'My mum's house is not even half as big and not half as chic, but it's cosy. That is my home.'

'I understand. It's nice to have a place where you feel at home.'

Simi nodded, and she remembered that Jay had spent most of his childhood at boarding school, with short vacations at his aunt's house. He had only spent time with his dad during the long holidays.

She smiled at him. 'I'm glad you came.'

Jay lay back on the sofa. 'I spoke to my dad this morning.'

Simi looked up sharply.

'No change,' he said. 'But the villagers are going to start clearing a path through the forest all the way to the lake today.'

'A path? Why?'

'For the tractors and lorries that will bring sand and gravel, of course!' Jay replied. 'They are going to fill up the lake in three days.'

'So soon? But . . . isn't anybody worried? I mean, who knows what will happen?' Simi felt a cold fear grip her.

'I thought that after what happened to Bubu, you would be relieved that they are filling it in. Are you worried about Oshun?'

'Well, yes, but it's not only that. It's . . .' Simi felt panic rising. If the lake was closed, her uncle would never come back . . .

She got up and began pacing the room. She suddenly realized quite clearly what she had to do.

'We have to go back.'

Jay's eyes widened. 'What?'

'I . . . I have to go back down there!'

He looked at her. 'Please do not tell me that "down there" means what I think it means.'

She nodded firmly, trying to look sure of herself, but she had to fold her hands into each other to stop them from trembling. 'I have to try to get my uncle out of there before the lake is filled up and closed for ever. And Morayo. She is not meant to be there.'

'Are you quite all right?' Jay asked. He looked really angry.

'I have to do it,' Simi said. 'I'm the only one who's ever come back from that place. There must be a reason why. This may sound strange, but I feel like it is my destiny to do this! I have to get them out of there!'

Jay jumped up. 'Stop it!' He was actually yelling now. 'I do not even want to hear this. It's like a really bad joke!'

'I'm not joking,' she said, in a low but steady voice. 'Until recently, I never believed in supernatural things. Especially not in goddesses and other worlds. But I saw that place with my own eyes. I was there!'

'Yes, and precisely because you *were* there, you must realize how real the danger is. Have you forgotten what happened to Bubu? We do not know if she will ever be herself again!'

Simi felt her belly tighten. 'The more reason for me to go. Maybe I can find out how to help her. If she is under a spell, maybe I can break the spell or find a cure or something.'

Jay was looking at her as if she was not only deluded but stupid too.

'Listen, what I believe in,' Simi went on, 'is fate! I believe that some things happen for a reason. That there is a greater sense behind everything. A bigger plan. I think it is no coincidence that I was sent to Ajao. Exactly when the lake was to be filled in. My mother, even though she was so traumatized by her past that she never wanted to go back, suddenly decided to send me there. Why now? When all these things are happening?'

Jay shook his head decisively. 'No. I'm sorry. No way.'

Simi looked at him with a sad smile. 'I will go back. Even without you. I have to, do you under-stand? It is . . . my role in this story.'

'What if you get stuck there and can never come back? Like the hundreds before you?'

'That is the risk I will have to take.'

'You want to risk your life for a "feeling"?'

'I'm not. I'm doing it for my uncle, for Bubu and Morayo. And for my mum. Don't you under-stand? My mum is only half of herself. She has been that way for as long as I can remember. She is terrified of water, and that something could happen to me. She probably hasn't slept well this past week, not knowing if I am OK. She carries a heavy sack full of remorse and guilt around with her all the time. She is not a happy person. She ran away from Ajao, from her past, because she could not bear the fact that her brother disappeared in the quicksands. She blames herself.'

Simi sat down beside him. 'Jay, I have to do this! I have to help if I can. That bird . . . it haunts me.'

Jay took a deep breath. Simi saw that his fingers were trembling, just like hers. 'Simi, listen to me,' he said urgently. 'You've probably also suffered some kind of trauma. You went through something scary and terrible and you feel responsible for what happened to Bubu. You just need time to get over it. Just wait a few days. Keep busy and think of something else. I could come and visit every day and we'll do things to keep your mind off things.'

Simi shook her head decisively. 'I do not have time to waste. You said it yourself. I have only three days. If the lake is filled in, I'll never forgive myself for not having tried.' She grabbed his arm. 'Please, Jay, help me. I . . . I do not want to end up like my mum. Full of regret.'

He pulled his hands out of her grasp and got up, shaking his head. 'Simi, you can't ask me to do that. That's unfair. I might be helping you to your death. I can't do that.'

'I am going to get on a bus to Ajao tonight.'

'I'll wait here until your dad comes home from work and tell him what you're up to.'

'He's in Port Harcourt.'

Jay flung himself into the chair in front of her and folded his arms across his chest.

'Jay, please. Come with me. I'm scared of travelling halfway across the country on my own.'

He snorted. 'You're afraid to travel alone by bus, but you're not afraid to plunge into a forbidden lake from which no one else has ever returned?' He shook his head in disbelief. 'Do you have any idea what my life will be like if something happens to you? What will I tell Iyanla or my dad?'

Simi nodded. 'You're right. I'm sorry I asked you. It is too much to ask of someone and it's not fair to you.'

He looked at her hopefully, but she added, 'I will have to manage without you. I'll be fine.'

24

The Return

At the last bus stop before Ajao, where Simi had said goodbye to her mum a week ago, the weather changed. It was as if the world was ending here. As if the sun had not even bothered to rise; in any case, it would have stood no chance against the angry rain.

Simi glanced at Jay as they waited for the taxi. He had hardly spoken to her on the entire trip but she was grateful that he had decided to come with her. Even if he was angry with her.

They were waiting in a hall, away from the rain, but it was cold and smelt of stale air and goats, and had a leak in the roof. Since no one was allowed to know about their arrival or their plan,

Jay had not called his father to send Moktar.

A young man who had been sleeping there ran off to wake the taxi driver, saying he would be back *now-now*. He came back with him two hours later.

The five steps from the hall to the taxi were enough to soak them from top to bottom. Wet and shivering, they jumped into the car. Simi pulled a long-sleeved T-shirt out of her rucksack and pulled it over her wet top, annoyed she hadn't packed a sweater. Her trainers were soaked and her socks made squelching noises as she moved her feet.

She immediately recognized the old driver who had brought her to Ajao the first time, Mr Balogun. The tattered taxi smelt even more strongly of goat this time, and Jay wrinkled his nose in disgust.

'Well, who's behaving like an ajebutter now?' Simi said with a tired grin.

Jay shrugged sulkily. He looked out of the window, his body tense.

'You again?' Mr Balogun asked, his stained teeth showing as he spoke. 'You don come visit Iyanla again?'

Simi nodded. She leant heavily against the door as he manoeuvred the taxi over potholes and along the road that was one big mudslide. The dark shadows of the trees looked like raging ghosts in the rain.

'Now no be good time to visit grandma. Iyanla don go Oshun shrine.'

'I know,' Simi replied.

'Iyanla never come back yet. E go hard to bring goddess to her senses,' he said. 'Goddess be woman. Woman always hard pass man to make happy when she vex.' He almost choked in a coughing fit of laughter at his own joke.

Simi rolled her eyes and looked across at Jay. But he didn't seem to be listening.

'Look at road. Too much water,' the driver went on. 'Look sky. Since Iyanla don go, the weather worse. And the river go burst soon. The farms dey shake with fear when dem see river.'

A firework of sharp flashes shot through the sky and deafening thunder followed.

'When Iyanla finish with Oshun, make she go greet Oya too. Oya don vex too.' Mr Balogun made a hissing sound and shook his head.

Hoping that he had stopped talking, Simi leant back in the seat. But he continued.

'This no be good time at all,' he said. 'Some men go to forbidden lake yesterday night with big trucks full with sand.'

'What?' Simi gasped. Jay looked up sharply.

'Big men don run away because of small bird. Small bird make big men fear.'

Simi pulled her arms across her chest to control the tremor that instantly passed through her body.

Jay shook his head but did not say anything.

Simi stared out of the window until exhaustion overcame her and her eyes closed.

The car came to a standstill with a loud rattle and Simi was startled awake. Iyanla's little house was in front of them. Somehow it looked even smaller as the heavy rain beat down on it. Simi's stomach lurched painfully at the thought of her plan. Being here suddenly made it real.

They thanked the driver and Simi paid with money Imona had given her. She had told Imona that she was visiting a friend and would be back by the weekend, when her dad would be back.

When Imona had offered to drive her to her friend's house, Simi had refused, saying she and Jay would share a taxi to get there.

Imona had looked very suspicious.

'I called Daddy this morning – he knows,' Simi had lied. 'He said he has money in his room and that you know where and should give me some.' Simi knew her father always kept a lot of cash in his room at home.

Imona nodded with a slightly irritated look but brought her the money.

Jay, in turn, had written his aunt a message, saying that he would be staying with a friend for a few days. Then they had both turned off their phones to escape any calls from their dads. They had stuffed some snacks into Simi's big rucksack along with her things.

Now she heaved the rucksack out of the car while Jay exchanged last words with the driver. She immediately glanced across the front yard to Mama Ayoola's house and thought of poor Bubu.

The dark forest loomed up behind the house. Her worries mingled with her fear and her fatigue, making her feel more awful than she ever remembered feeling before.

Inside the house, Simi lit a kerosene lantern and placed it on the table in the tiny living room. Then she grabbed two towels from the shelf in the corridor and handed one to Jay.

When they had rubbed themselves dry, Simi went out into the yard. She wanted to see if she could get the fire started to heat water for tea. The rain drummed forcefully on the corrugated-iron sheets of the outside roof, like a warning. Simi's chest rose and fell faster and she suddenly felt she was suffocating. She held on to one of the chairs and gasped for air.

You can't do this, a voice in her head said. But she ignored the voice and tried to calm down. She had to focus. She needed wood. Wood and . . . matches. Her hands were shaking terribly, and she did not know if it was the cold or the fear. She pushed some pieces of wood together, as Iyanla had shown her, and managed to get the fire going. She filled a little pot with water and placed it on the fire.

She tried to rub the cold out of her limbs while she watched the flames grow in size, but couldn't stop trembling. She tried to ignore the growing tightness in her belly and told herself to breathe deeply. But her breath came in a loud gasp just as Jay came outside.

'Hey!' he said, and looked at her in shock. 'Oh, my goodness, Simi. You're a complete wreck!'

He sat down in front of her and smiled kindly.

'Simi, you know you really don't have to do this.'

She wanted to nod and believe him. But she knew she would not be able to live with herself if she didn't do it. Tears welled up in her eyes. Jay glanced towards the house, biting his nails and avoiding her gaze.

'Simi, there is something I, erm . . . have to tell you. But please don't be angry with me.'

She stared at him, wondering what he meant, when he suddenly froze and cocked his head. He was listening for something.

'Someone is at the door,' he said, and went back into the house.

Simi tried to think, but was confused. Who was at the door? And what had Jay meant about not being angry at him?

She turned to look through the corridor and saw him open the door. A tall, thin figure under a black umbrella stood there. And as the figure lowered his head to come in, she recognized Moktar's turban. She immediately knew what Jay had done.

He had betrayed her.

He had called Moktar to help him stop her.

She had to go immediately. It was either now or never.

Simi stumbled through the herb garden, shuddering as the cold rain hit her face, and ripped open the small garden gate. She almost stopped at the sight of the roaring stream in front of her. It had tripled in size and its waters splashed over its banks, hissing and fighting the wind. Simi splashed to the left, taking the flooded path that led to the forest.

The darkness there was stifling. The wind howled in the treetops, and the whispering and rustling of thousands of wet leaves was awful. She stumbled as she ran along the narrow path, willing her legs to move faster. Creepers and thorns swiped at her as she ran. She heard calls behind her, and recognized Moktar's deep voice and Jay's frantic one. She knew Jay and Moktar would soon catch up with her, and a new wave of energy spun through her as she turned off the path on to the one that she knew would lead her to the forbidden lake.

When she arrived at the lake, the fear instilled into her by her mother almost made her stop. The first time she had waded into the lake, she had been enchanted by the bird. Now she would have to jump in of her own free will.

'Simi, don't!' Jay's voice was right behind her and she heard the despair in it.

'I'm sorry,' she called, forcing herself to take the last few steps and then leap on to the muddy shore. The only worry she had now was that he would follow her. She turned a moment before the water and the convulsing arms of the quicksands swallowed her. She saw Jay trying to jump in after her and Moktar grabbing him at the last moment and pinning him to the ground.

Simi inhaled one last gulp of air and allowed the cold whirl of the quicksands to take control.

25

The Other World

When the sands spat her out, Simi was so dizzy and queasy that she didn't know where up or down was. The sand was still making ugly smacking noises as she pulled her feet away and struggled out of its reach on to more solid ground.

The two rows of trembling sandhills separated by the path stretched out in front of her, and she knew she was in the other place. She wondered whether to hide in the crevice again or walk through the sandhills immediately to search for her uncle and Morayo. Before she could make a decision, she realized that it was too late: she had been discovered.

Two wiry-looking children ran up the path towards her. One was a girl of Simi's age. The other was a younger boy. Both of them, like the children on her previous visit, wore a rough, brown cloth and carried spears, with the sharp ends facing the sky. Simi stood rooted to the ground, not able to say or do anything.

The boy reacted first. He made a gesture for Simi to come towards them, and she automatically moved forward, then stopped and cleared her throat.

'I . . . um . . . I want to speak to Toyin,' she said. 'Is he here?'

The children looked at each other, then shook their heads.

'No?' she asked. 'No, I can't speak to him? Or no, he is not here?'

The children glanced at each other again but still said nothing.

'I have to speak to him urgently.' She folded her arms. 'I will not go anywhere if I do not speak to him.'

The children glanced at each other a third time.

'This one wants trouble,' said the boy now,

breaking his silence. He spoke with that weird emphasis that had struck her the last time – as if all sentences were being asked as questions.

'She does not know what it means to upset Layo,' the girl said in a sharp, high-pitched voice.

'We have to make her understand,' the boy said.

The girl nodded and turned the tip of her spear towards Simi until it touched her neck.

Simi felt her heart beat faster and a sudden pressure in her throat. She swallowed carefully.

'Maybe she will finally get moving?' the girl said. But her eyes were on Simi's neck. In a movement so swift that Simi could not even react, the girl tore Iyanla's necklace from her.

'Ouch!' Simi yelled. 'You could have asked politely, and I might have taken the necklace off and given it to you. But, come to think of it, I probably wouldn't have. I would *not* have given it to you, because I got it from my grandmother and it is *mine*!' She glared at the girl.

In an almost elegant movement, the girl again pressed the spear into Simi's neck. This time it definitely hurt. 'She will say nothing more.' The girl hid the necklace in the folds of her cloth and then made a motion with her head for Simi to move.

'But will Sister Temitope not get into trouble because she has claimed something from a new-one?'

'Who will tell anybody?' the girl asked sharply.

The boy did not reply but took a step behind Simi and nudged her on with one finger. 'Will the new-one move, please?'

Reluctantly, Simi did as he asked. But as she walked between them through the strange landscape, she tried again. 'I just came here to speak to Toyin, you know. I am not planning on staying here.'

Sister Temitope turned and looked at her. 'Brother Dapo,' she said, without taking her gaze off Simi, 'this one does not get it. This new-one is like a hard palm nut that is difficult to crack.'

'Yes, this new-one is tough,' the boy agreed.

'It's you both who are being difficult,' Simi said, annoyed. 'And why are you talking about me as if I am air?'

As the path began to curve around the hills, a

pretty, frail-looking face peeped out. It was a girl with large, worried eyes.

'Another new-one?' she whispered. 'So soon? How come?'

'Get away from here, Sister Morayo!' Sister Temitope cried angrily.

'Sister Morayo?' Simi called. 'Morayo, is it you who came here some months ago?'

Morayo nodded sadly.

'I want to help you,' Simi called, but was interrupted by Sister Temitope.

'You know you shouldn't be here!'

Morayo's face scrunched up in fear and she disappeared out of sight.

Simi walked faster, trying to catch up with her. But when they reached the end of the path, Simi stopped mid-stride.

Ahead lay dark grey plains and drooping, withered plants. Thick, red, murky trails that looked like smoking lava snaked across the land, covering and suffocating everything in their way. The plants and trees were stranger than anything Simi had seen before.

'What is this?' she asked fearfully, not daring to

go a step further. A smoking puddle blocked the path in front of them. There was no sight of Morayo.

The boy looked around, his eyes flitting nervously. 'It is the evil,' he whispered. 'It was not always like this.'

The girl slapped the back of his head. 'Shut up! Do you want to get us into trouble?' Then she turned to Simi. 'Move, new-one!'

The path curved away out of view and got lost in distant dark fields covered with snaking red rivers. Between them, she saw children carrying baskets on their heads. They looked wretched and tired.

Simi cupped her hands around her mouth. 'Toyin! Morayo!' she called as loud as she could.

Her voice echoed, and it seemed as if the dark red puddle in front of her began to sizzle and smoke even more.

'What are you doing?' the boy hissed. His eyes were wide with shock. 'Do you want to awaken those who should not be awakened?'

Suddenly a deeper boy's voice yelled back, 'Who is shouting in my ear like this? Show your face!'

Simi stiffened and noticed both children beside her turn equally rigid. The girl pushed her forward while the boy grabbed her hand and pulled her through the smoking puddle. Simi flinched, expecting to get burnt, but the thick murk just sizzled away from her feet, only spreading a nasty rotten smell.

The path turned once more and Simi found herself in front of the largest tree she had ever seen, the grey plains stretching away behind it.

It was an iroko, a tree of spirits – like the one at the forbidden lake, but its trunk was so thick that if she'd tried to stretch her arms around it, they wouldn't even begin to curve. Strange vines hung down from its branches like long red snakes, and hanging between them was a swing – an intricately carved throne attached to the thickest vines. On it sat a strong-looking boy, his bare feet dangling. He had a handsome face, with even features and beautiful dark skin that glowed. He wore a rough black cloth knotted over his shoulder and in his hand he carried a long horse-tail whisk. Simi felt very nervous.

'Sister Temitope and Brother Dapo have

brought a new-one,' the girl said.

'I'm not a new-one,' Simi said quickly. 'My name is Simi and I'm not staying. I only came to speak to—'

The boy on the swing threw his head back and laughed. Tendrils of dark red smoke curled up from the ground, seeping into the boy's bare dangling feet.

'This new-one is amusing!'

Simi couldn't help feeling a jolt of anger. 'I am happy to see that my presence is amusing! But I am only here to look for some . . . erm . . . some friends, and as soon as I have found them, I will be out of here!'

At her words, there was a gust of wind. From the corner of her eye Simi saw something move swiftly towards them, leaving a dusty streak in the sky. Dark grey wings appeared out of nowhere and a bird settled on the ground directly in front of her. There was a golden glitter among its feathers and she knew instantly that it was the magic bird that had called her twice now.

At once the two children grabbed her shoulders and pushed her to her knees. It was easy because her legs had weakened and felt like water. Simi peeked through her braids, which had fallen forward, covering her face.

The bird's eyes were black and looked straight into hers. Her reflection in its eyes was smoky and distorted. The boy had stopped swinging and was watching the bird's every move – its head cocking to stare at Simi and its rustling feathers that showed the gold glitter in its wings. Golden streaks began to appear in the boy's own dark hair. He tightened his grip on his throne and leant forward.

'Does the new-one know who she is facing?'

Simi answered in a trembling voice, 'You are Layo?'

The bird flew up on to Layo's shoulder and made an impatient low sound. Layo tilted his head towards it, without taking his eyes off Simi. The bird chirped softly into his ear and Layo's eyes widened and his face broke into a smile.

Simi scrambled up and took a step back as the boy king jumped off the swing. With a quick jerk, he grabbed her wrist. She felt small and helpless in front of him. He was a head taller than she was.

Still holding her wrist, Layo turned her around, admiring her as if she were a trophy. 'So this is the one who has been here before! The one whose return we have been waiting for!'

Sister Temitope glared at Simi as if she was an imposter. Simi noticed how both she and Brother Dapo carefully avoided looking at the bird, which had perched on the swing and was now strutting around with tiny jerky steps.

'Gather everyone at the lake,' Layo suddenly shouted.

The children jumped.

'Quick!' he barked at them.

They scuttled off.

Simi's thoughts were running wild. What was happening and what did all this mean? Like so many times before, she wondered why she was the only one to have ever left this place. She had not done anything special: she had just jumped back into the lake and the quicksands had carried her back. Why had the other children not simply done the same?

Everything here was desolate and ruined; it was not the beautiful place of the legend. Iyanla had said Oshun had created a paradise for Layo and the children. Something was very wrong. The bird was the one in control, she realized. Had it ruined this place?

Simi edged away. Could she try to disappear and go in search of Toyin and Morayo? She didn't feel safe here with Layo and the bird.

But the moment she slipped away around the corner, she heard a loud rush of wings behind her and a scream so shrill and piercing that she held her hands to her ears. A shredding sound cut through the silence that followed. Simi turned and saw the bird burst out of its feathers. Its wings stretched out to a huge width and grey dust puffed out of its body, darkening the air. Its eyes sparkled golden as it floated above her.

Layo came up beside her, his eyes as golden as the bird's. 'Nobody can do anything if we do not allow it!' he said. 'Has the new-one that calls herself Simi understood?'

Simi nodded quickly. The bird slowly shrank back to its former size. Grey dust filled the air and Simi began to cough, her eyes burning.

Crowds of children began to come up from the

grey plains, trudging past them. Heads bowed and eyes listless, they didn't even look up as they passed.

Layo grabbed Simi's arm and pulled her in the direction of the sandhills.

'To the lake,' he said.

And he was so strong that Simi had no choice but to stumble after him on shaky legs.

26

Hopeless

Hundreds of children were sitting on the quivering hills overlooking the lake. But it was as quiet as a graveyard. The children watched Simi with faces tense and alert, as she was dragged along the soft, red path between the hills, trying to avoid the smoky red puddles that appeared everywhere.

'Simi will tell them!' Layo hissed.

'T-tell them what?' she stuttered.

He frowned. 'Tell them about the bird! Tell them what she has done in the overworld!'

'Erm . . . well . . . I do not know . . . but a child has been called to the quicksands who should not have been called.'

He let out an impatient snort. 'Yes! But tell them why she did it. Tell them how the goddesses are fighting in the overworld because of that! Tell them how waters are fighting with the winds!'

Simi stared at him. Did he mean that the bird had deliberately lured Morayo down here to cause the fight between the goddesses? But why?

The children were silent, waiting. And it looked like they were afraid of her answer.

'True or not?' Layo asked sharply, turning to face her.

Simi nodded carefully. 'Well . . . yes . . .' she began.

The bird was circling low above them, her small, elegant head held proudly high, her feathers glittering against the dark sky, before she landed on Layo's shoulder once more.

'Why?' Simi asked, trying hard to be brave though she felt anything but. 'Why is she causing the goddesses to argue?'

'She says Oshun has no right to keep children here for ever.' Layo stretched out his hand to the crowds on the hills. 'All these children have no right to be here. We do not have the right to live for ever! That is why she caused the quarrel between the goddesses. She wants Oya to force Oshun to close the quicksands world.'

Simi gasped. What did that mean for all these children? She shook her head. 'No. Oshun is the goddess of water, the essence of life. She loves children and would never agree to that! She made a beautiful world so that the children would have a wonderful place to live for ever!'

The bird clucked softly, her beak almost touching the boy's face. The golden streaks glowed in his hair. Layo smiled.

'Simi is right. Oshun is stubborn and has not agreed to Oya's demands. And that is why it is good that *Simi* has come.'

Simi felt a cold fear spread through her body.

'Simi will lead us out of here,' Layo said.

Simi gasped in relief. Well, that was the first piece of good news she had heard since she arrived! She was very willing to get them all out of here and save them from this dying place. Her heart warmed at the thought of bringing her uncle back to her mum and Iyanla, and Morayo back to her father. She looked around, relieved. But why were the children on the hills whispering fearfully among themselves. Why did they not look happy?

A boy Simi immediately recognized as Brother Dapo cautiously began to speak. 'Has Layo forgotten that Oshun gave us this gift of immortality? She gave us a wonderful home where we never suffer, never hunger, never have pain, where we could live happily for ever. Our world was not always ruined like this. Has Layo forgotten?'

'We were happy here before this evil bird came and ruined our world!' someone else called.

'We don't want to go back to the overworld! Don't listen to the evil one. She was born out of the eggshell of darkness, in the land of the Egun spirits. She is pure evil!' another child cried.

'We don't want our world destroyed!'

'We don't want to go! We don't want to go!'

The children began to slide down the hills, shouting. The bird spread her wings stiffly and began to trill. There was a crackling sound and the hills began to shudder even more. Then they split open beneath the children and thick red liquid spilt out of the dark crevices.

The children struggled back up, screaming. The

bird circled the hills, wings outstretched, as if daring anyone to make another move or say another word.

Simi stared at the bird in shock, limbs trembling.

Layo glanced grimly at Simi and walked towards her.

'I . . . I do not want to lead anyone out if they don't want it!' Simi said. Her voice was shaky and small, and she took a step backwards.

'Simi will lead us out of here. Layo will go first!'

Layo grabbed her arm and pulled her into the water. Her feet sank a few centimetres into the soft sand and the smooth red surface rippled softly.

Then he jumped into the lake, dragging her with him.

The cold water quickly pulled her down and Simi held her breath, waiting for the usual suction and whirl that would spin her around and then spit her out into the forest of Ajao. But nothing happened.

The panic rose in Simi and she felt her lungs begin to tighten. She tried frantically to pull her hand out of Layo's grip. Her lungs felt like they would burst. She tried to swim upwards towards the surface of the water. But Layo's grip on her hand was like iron. She wriggled and pulled, but he was merciless. In her panic, she began to gasp for air and choked. Water penetrated her lungs and she choked more. In a final attempt to free herself, she tried to bite his arm but he still did not let go. A terrible pain overcame her lungs as she gasped and convulsed. She fought for her life but already felt the strength leave her muscles. When he finally pulled her upwards, she had almost lost consciousness.

With a thud her body hit the bank of the lake. She felt something jerking and heard someone cough. It took her a while to realize that it was her body that was jerking and that she was coughing and gasping for air. And then a burning pain set in that felt like it would tear her lungs apart. But before she could even breathe in enough air to fill her lungs, someone pushed her over. She rolled on to her back and saw Layo towering above her.

'What was that?' he yelled. 'Why did Simi do that?'

Simi moaned and tried to pull herself up on to her elbows. Hundreds of nervous eyes watched her from above.

'Why did she do that?' Layo repeated.

'I—' Simi had another coughing fit and spat out water. 'I don't know. Last time it was different.'

The bird fluttered in panic around them.

'Simi is trying to trick us,' Layo shouted.

But Simi was not listening, because a gruesome realization had just shot through her mind. She now understood the truth of the situation she was in.

The quicksands had not carried her back to her world. She could not leave this place. There was nothing she could do for anyone here, so she had endangered herself for nothing. She should have listened to Jay. Now she would have to stay here in this ruined world, the entrance to be destroyed any moment by the villagers.

She had to try again. If only she could get back and find Iyanla. Warn her about what was happening. Her grandmother could talk to Oshun, tell her what the bird had done, and the goddess could help save the quicksands world.

She stumbled to her feet and Layo immediately gripped her wrist. Not caring that she had not fully recovered, she jumped in with him again.

Again she waited for the current and the whirling, and again it did not come.

In her desperation, she tried to dive deeper. Layo swam down to the bottom with her. But even at the bottom of the lake, nothing happened. She dug one hand desperately into the sand and swirled the slimy clay around but nothing happened.

When she ran out of breath and wanted to swim back up, Layo held her down. She wriggled and pulled in panic, gasping, swallowing water, thinking again that her lungs would burst and she would die. It seemed to take for ever before Layo finally released her.

Wet, desperate and exhausted, she collapsed on the bank of the lake. Tears mingled with the water streaming down her face. She gasped and coughed and cried, not caring that hundreds were watching her.

Even the bird did not scare her any more. Nothing was as horrible as the thought of never being able to go back to her world, never seeing her mum again, never seeing her dad, her friends or Iyanla again.

'She will try again.' She heard Layo's voice echo through her thoughts. But she hardly noticed anything around her.

Like in a dream where she barely felt her limbs, she struggled up and fell back into the water with him. She felt such a deep sadness in her chest that the pain in her lungs did not seem so bad. She did not even fight it any more. All she could think of was how she would break her mum's heart a second time. And she knew that this time her mum would not survive it.

When she came back to herself, she was on the bank once more. She felt hands gently massaging her back. Little hands stroking her forehead and a soft, whispering voice trying to console her.

She opened her eyes and found herself looking into a strangely familiar face. It was creased with worry, but she immediately recognized the little boy from Iyanla's old photo.

Toyin.

'Simi looks so much like Biola,' the boy said softly. 'Why did Simi come here? Biola will be so sad to lose her daughter as well.' His face looked very troubled. 'Toyin made Biola and his mother very sad already.'

Another figure knelt beside him. It was the frail-looking girl from the path. Morayo.

'Simi should not have come,' she whispered. 'There is no hope for us.' Her large eyes were kind but very sad.

'Is she awake?' Simi heard Layo's voice.

Toyin nodded, but did not take his eyes off her face.

'She will try again,' she heard Layo say. 'Again and again and again. Until it works.'

This time a hushed murmur went through the crowd of children.

Toyin shook his head. 'She cannot, and just because Layo tries again and again, it will not change the fact that it will not work.'

'What?' Layo's voice hardened.

Toyin stood in front of Simi. 'She cannot! Simi is my family and I will protect her,' he said.

A shadow swerved over them and Simi heard the familiar rush of wings, followed by an agonized screech. Toyin ducked his head as the bird swept over them and then began to circle. Her feathers turned from gold to black to gold once more.

'Away with him!' Layo yelled. 'Nobody will stand in our way!'

27

A Drop of Blue

Simi's stomach churned, the red puddles sizzled loudly and the air was filled with glistening red fog.

She swallowed painfully. She felt battered and weak.

'Come, Brother Toyin,' Sister Temitope whispered. 'Don't make things worse than they already are.' The girl placed a hand gently on Toyin's arm and in that moment Simi noticed a tiny flash of clear blue beneath the knot of cloth at her neck.

Her necklace with the blue stone!

In that instant she realized that this could be her last strand of hope. Her way home! 'My necklace!' she exclaimed. 'I was wearing my necklace with the blue stone the first time I came. Sister Temitope took it from me. That may be the reason! Maybe the stone is magic.'

Sister Temitope glanced frantically at the bird, who was again perched on Layo's shoulder.

Layo turned slowly, his eyes dark. 'Sister Temitope took something from a new-one? Something she did not show Layo?'

Sister Temitope removed the chain from her neck with trembling hands. Simi immediately felt sorry for her.

Layo cocked his head to listen to the bird's excited chirping.

'This changes everything,' he said. 'If we have a magic talisman, then we will not need Simi any more!'

Simi's knees weakened.

'Bring me the talisman, and away with Simi,' he ordered.

Sister Temitope moved forward slowly, the necklace dangling from her trembling hand.

Simi watched the stone, her last ray of hope, being carried away. Its intense greenish-blue looked strangely liquid. A sudden warm feeling overcame her. She felt as if she was staring into the very depths of a warm river on a sunny day. She could see the faint rippling of water within the stone, as if a gentle breeze was inside it. Almost in a trance she moved towards the stone, drawn by its depth and by an overwhelming sense that it couldn't fall into the wrong hands.

She stretched out her hand and snatched it from Sister Temitope.

The moment the greenish-blue stone touched her palm, its colour flared up. The stone in her hand felt natural, reassuring, like a part of her that had been missing. Its warmth seeped into her body and she felt strong and bold.

'It is mine, given to me by my grandmother, Iyanla, priestess of the goddess Oshun!' she cried.

Strange sensations like waves of water rolled through her arms, but they did not feel awkward. They felt like a long-lost part of her.

There were gasps from the children on the hill-tops and a dark cloud of screeching feathers flew towards her at full speed. Simi stood her ground, pressed her fist clasping the stone against her chest and closed her eyes. She knew instinctively that she had Oshun's protection. Her grandmother's strength. And her mother's love. She had the power of all of Oshun's daughters in her.

When the bird tried to snatch the stone, there was a burst of blue light that Simi sensed even through her closed eyes. Then a desperate struggle of wings and claws and a frenzied beating of feathers. A terrible, agonized scream that echoed across the hills. And silence.

Simi opened her eyes gingerly. A large blue bubble floated in the air in front of her. In its centre was a smoky-grey bundle of feathers.

Layo stared at the bubble, looking confused and pale. The golden streaks were fading from his hair.

'Mama,' he cried, his eyes filling with tears.

Inside the bubble the bird stopped struggling. Its beady eyes, fixed on Layo, had lost their wicked glint and were filled with sadness.

Simi stared in shock. The bird was Adunni – Layo's mother!

Adunni, the woman in the legend who had refused to have another child because she would not share her love for Layo. The woman whom everyone had warned against too much love. She had escaped from the Egun, from Oya's world of the dead, to return her son to the living, so that one day they would be united.

'Mama, I know you wish we could be together again, and so do I, but what you did was not right! This place is my home now. These children are my family. You can't hurt everyone here just because of me. That is not love, Mama.'

At that, the bird's dark feathers began to bristle and, ever so gently, she stretched out the tip of her wing towards Layo.

A cool breeze blew past Simi. She shivered and rubbed her arms. The winds of Oya had come to carry Adunni home.

'Goodbye, Mama,' Layo whispered, as the winds lifted the bubble.

The bird was fading and almost transparent now and its beautiful shape glistened, one wing still stretched towards Layo.

As the bubble floated away, water began to leak from it, spreading over the red sand in all directions. Thin blue streams met the smoking red puddles, which retreated as if in fear and disappeared into the ground.

Layo stared after the spirit of his mother vanishing into the sky, which was already clearing. He fell to his knees, trembling. His hair was a glossy black once more, free from the gold of his mother's spell. They were all free.

Some children slid down the hills and hurried towards him. 'Kpele, Layo,' they whispered. 'So sorry, Layo.'

Simi let out a sad sigh.

Suddenly, there were shouts and happy cries and she turned to look. The streams from the bubble had spread a blue glow which now drifted beyond the hills. It was damp and refreshing, like morning dew, and it spread everywhere, driving away the red fog and healing the world of the quicksands.

Simi held the stone tightly, feeling its warmth. She could feel Oshun's presence. The warmth that radiated out of the blue stone and into this world was her.

'Thank you, Sister Simi!'

Some children watched her with wide eyes.

Sister Temitope and Brother Dapo threw down their spears and ran past her. They scrambled up to the top of the nearest hill to see the landscape beyond. Simi climbed up after them. And then stared in awe at the beauty that lay spread out in front of her.

The entire world was in blossom. Thousands of trees and plants, laden with fruit or dotted with flowers. She had never seen so many plants blooming at the same time and she didn't recognize a single one. The red puddles were all gone, the plants grew tall and straight, no longer withered. On some of the trees hung blue hairy fruits! A clear blue river curved through the fields and orchards, glittering in the bright light.

It was absolutely beautiful and she couldn't believe she was standing right in the middle of it.

Overcome with relief, Simi sat down on the soft sand. The strange quivering hills gave her a feeling of what sitting in a boat on the Lagos Lagoon might be like. The constant gentle sway was calming. This was the quicksands world as it was meant to be.

She watched the children slide down the hillsides

and run along the soft path towards the blossoming orchards, their faces full of laughter.

Some children helped Layo up. 'Come and see, Layo,' they said. 'Come and see.'

A crystal-clear child's voice began to sing in the distance and children's voices from all around joined in the song. They were singing for Oshun. Simi felt overwhelmed by the joy and beauty around her. She touched the stone once more, feeling its warmth and power.

'Thank you!' she whispered.

28

Time for Goodbyes

Toyin climbed up the hill and sat down beside Simi. She couldn't help staring at him, still surprised that he looked just like he did in the old photo.

'So Simi is also a priestess of Oshun, like Iyanla?' Toyin asked with a smile.

'Oh, I am not a priestess! I was just wearing the priestess's stone around my neck!'

'Only a true priestess can draw on the power of the goddess,' Toyin said.

Simi felt goosebumps at the memory of the strange blue energy that had pulsed through the necklace, into her veins and out of her.

She shrugged. 'Well, luckily I arrived in Ajao

just when all this began to happen and Iyanla gave me her necklace.'

'Everything has a reason!' Toyin said. 'No one but a child could have entered this world, and no one but a priestess of Oshun could have summoned her power to help us. Only you could have done this. Only you could free our world from Adunni.'

Simi nodded. That was the feeling she had had all along.

'What now?' she asked Toyin.

Toyin did not reply immediately. He looked thoughtful.

When he turned to face her, she saw that his eyes were filled with sadness.

'Why do I have the feeling that it is time for goodbyes?' Simi asked. 'You will not come back with me?' Her heart felt heavy.

Toyin shook his head. 'I wish I could, because of Biola and Iyanla. But I can't. Like Layo, I belong here.'

Simi knew he was right, though it hurt to accept it.

'Apart from Morayo, who was lured here by

Adunni against her will, every single one of us is meant to be here and happy to stay. Oshun is kind. Look at our world. It is perfect again!' Toyin pointed at the orchards in the distance.

'For thousands of years, children with no family and no place to go have been coming here. They had felt close to Oshun all their life, like I did, and it was like coming home.'

Simi pondered this. She had sensed all along that the goddess wasn't cruel; she was saving the children who came into this world from a sad existence. 'But why did *you* come here? Were you not happy?' she asked her uncle.

'It is difficult to explain in my case,' he said, scratching his head. 'Every person has a spirit side. Some have it more, some less. Maybe it's because Iyanla is so close to Oshun – maybe that is why the spirit part of me was so strong. I always felt very close to Oshun. My whole life in the overworld, I felt I didn't belong. The world up there was not my home. And I think Iyanla always knew it.'

He paused and his eyes brimmed with tears. 'I managed to stay there for Biola all those years, but then I just had to leave. I was never meant to be born into the overworld. My heart was always here.' He touched his heart and then touched the thick red soil beside him. He covered her hand with his small hand and pressed gently. 'Please tell Iyanla that Toyin will always carry her in his heart. And that he asks forgiveness for running away.'

He took a wooden object out of a little pouch attached to a raffia belt around his waist. 'Please give Biola this. Tell her that all these years it made Toyin remember her and it made him happy. Now he wants her to remember him and be happy too.'

Simi looked at the object in her palm. It was a little car carved out of wood – the one Toyin had been holding in Iyanla's old photo. She nodded as tears filled her eyes. Then she held him in a tight hug.

They walked back to the lake together and found Morayo was already there, waiting.

The sands convulsed and churned and spat Simi and Morayo out into a calm forest. The trees that had been swaying aggressively as howling winds tore at their crowns were now still and peaceful. The rains that had beaten down in torrents had ceased.

Iyanla's slim figure stood in the middle of the path. Her face was turned upwards to the sky. She wore her white wrapper and her legs were decorated with efun patterns. Her face and chest were divided in half. The half that was painted white was smudged by the rain. Her grey hair was intricately woven and adorned with cowrie shells.

Behind her Simi saw Jay and Moktar hiding in the shadows.

When Iyanla spotted Simi and Morayo, she raised her hands and called out strange words that Simi did not understand. Immediately, a huge tornado formed and circled around them. It passed over them and hovered directly over the lake, like a narrow tunnel leading up to the sky.

Morayo slipped a trembling hand into Simi's and they watched wide-eyed as the water from the lake began to rise. Oshun and Oya worked hand in hand; water and wind were reconciled. Large waves formed, reaching upwards out of the lake like outstretched arms. The waves were sucked up through the vortex of the tornado and disappeared with a rushing sound up into the white clouds. The clouds swelled, turned grey and then white, and lifted, showing a clear blue sky.

Simi stared at what had once been the lake.

Like a reflection of the quicksands world – at once the same and yet so different – a garden-like oasis had sprung up where the lake had lain for thousands of years. Banana, paw-paw, cashew and orange trees stood heavily laden as if they were in season, and juicy, ripe pineapples grew at their base. Bright flowers and rare grasses covered the ground and monkeys swung through the trees, chittering loudly. The iroko tree and the rock were the only things that made the spot recognizable.

Jay let out a quiet gasp and came out of hiding. He grabbed Simi into a hug. 'I am so glad you are safe!' he said. 'Welcome back! Morayo, right?' he asked, smiling at Morayo. She nodded, beaming at him.

Simi smiled at him and then watched him gingerly enter the garden, his jaw dropping in awe.

Iyanla let out a tired sigh. 'It is done,' she said. Then she leant over, breathing heavily. 'Simi.'

Simi ran forward and Iyanla put her arms around her.

Simi looked anxiously at her grandmother. 'Iyanla, I saw Toyin and the other children. With the magic of Oshun's stone, we stopped Adunni.' Her words came in short bursts.

Iyanla nodded as if she already knew all of it.

'The goddess sisters have come to an agreement,' she said. 'Oshun has allowed Oya to dry up the lake for ever. No more children will disappear. She has agreed that the correct way of things is not for people to live eternally. Even if Oshun loves her children, as from now, she has to let them follow the normal path of life and death. And, in turn, Oya has agreed to strengthen the gates to the Egun to make sure the spirits stay with their ancestors, as they should.

'The goddesses were so busy quarrelling and blaming each other that they did not notice what was happening in the quicksands world. It was only when you wielded Oshun's power through the stone that Oshun saw what Adunni had done and ended the quarrel.'

Iyanla looked at Simi, her eyes glinting. 'You did well, my child.' Simi felt immensely proud.

'Morayo, it is a happy day to see that you are back. You have been badly missed by your family and everyone,' Iyanla added.

'It is weird, but I can hear voices even though there is no one here,' Jay called.

Simi listened and also had a strange feeling she could hear chattering as well as the wind in the leaves. Even some laughter.

Iyanla nodded. 'It is a reminder from the goddess, so that the children of the quicksands will never be forgotten.'

She looked at Simi directly now. 'Is he well? My son?'

'Yes, he is! He is in a wonderful place.'

Iyanla nodded slowly.

'He said to tell you that he carries you in his heart always and asks you to forgive him for running away.'

Iyanla stared at the spot where the lake had once been. A tear rolled down the white chalky pattern on her cheek as she listened to the distant sound of children's voices.

'You have been forgiven, my son. Long ago already,' she whispered. 'May the goddess keep you safe.'

29

Grandmothers, Mothers and Daughters

There was a big commotion in front of Iyanla's house. The whole village, and even people from other villages, had gathered. The news had travelled fast that Iyanla's granddaughter had jumped into the lake and returned with Morayo. People wanted to see for themselves if it was true.

Morayo and her father were surrounded by a crowd of excited people. Baba Morayo had held Simi's hand so tightly when thanking her that she thought he would never let go.

And to Simi's amazement, Bubu suddenly rushed out of Mama Ayoola's house, followed by a man and a woman.

'Gently, Bubu, gently!' the woman said with a smile.

'Simi, my parents came home when they heard I was ill! I knew it. I knew bushbaby didn't take my dad away! Isn't that amazing?' Bubu was more excited than Simi had ever seen her. There was not a single sign in her smiling face that she had spent three days in a trance.

Simi greeted Bubu's parents and hugged Bubu tightly.

'I knew they would come back. I mean, who believes such stupid stories about snakes and bushbabies anyway!' Bubu said, with an absolutely innocent look on her face.

Simi grinned.

'Is it true that the bird that called me also called you with its evil magic song? Did you actually go inside the lake and did you actually see . . .'

Mama Ayoola appeared at that moment and hugged Bubu and Simi together, and there was enough space for them both. She had happy tears in her eyes.

'Bubu, allow Simi some rest. And you should also go and lie down a bit.'

Bubu allowed her parents to take her away, and Simi sighed as she thought how much the villagers had suffered because of what Adunni had done. Even though Oshun had meant the world beneath the lake to be a good place, it had caused pain to many.

The chief arrived with some men, and Jay took him and a crowd of villagers back to the lake to show them the beautiful garden it had now become.

Mama Ayoola boiled a bitter-sweet tea in Iyanla's largest pot and began handing out cups of tea.

As Simi was changing into dry clothes, she heard Bubu's voice outside – loud, excited and without any of her usual shyness or fear. She obviously had not gone to bed as Mama Ayoola had suggested.

'I was just sitting peacefully, minding my business and not speaking a single word because it was after four o'clock in the afternoon, when I heard this strange whistling song. And all of a sudden my legs began doing what they felt like! They just started walking me into the forest. And then, up in the trees, I saw the bird with my own koro-koro eyes!'

'Oh, my goodness! Were you not afraid?' some-one asked.

Simi stepped out of the house to see that a huge circle of people had formed around Bubu. Her eyes were wide and sparkling, and her plaits stood more upright than ever.

'Well, I was, but since my legs were not listen-ing to me, there was nothing I could do about it.' Bubu drew a circle above her head with her right hand and snapped her fingers to fend off evil. 'God forbid bad thing,' she muttered.

'Well, now that the lake is dried up, the chil-dren of the quicksands are lost for ever,' Kikelomo sighed sadly.

'The children of the quicksands will live for ever!' Simi replied, even though she felt somewhat sad. 'It is the most beautiful place I have ever seen,' she added.

All of a sudden the crowd opened. 'What nonsense!' a strangely familiar voice called. Simi flinched in surprise, then in recognition and finally in shock.

Her mum pushed through the crowd.

'Mum, what are you doing here? Why are you not in London?' Simi cried.

'Ah! Who am I seeing? Is that Biola? What a day this is,' Mama Ayoola called.

Her mum was breathing heavily and did not notice anyone else. 'We are leaving this place immediately. I was worried sick when your dad called me saying you had left secretly and had probably headed back here. Luckily, after your phone call, I had already cancelled my training and booked the next flight back to Lagos. I could feel something was wrong. Quick, get your things. We are leaving right now!'

'But, Mum, please listen . . . something happened. I saw Uncle Toyin!'

Simi lowered her voice. The whole crowd was watching and listening.

Her mum's face turned stony. 'Simi, stop it! I knew it was a bad mistake to send you here. Pack your things!'

Suddenly, her mum went rigid. She was staring past Simi and looked like she had seen a ghost. Simi turned to find Iyanla standing behind her.

'Biola!' Iyanla's voice was low. 'It makes an old woman happy to see her daughter.'

'Mama!' Biola began, her face softening. But then her gaze hardened. 'I had somehow hoped that things would have changed here.'

'But, Mum, it is true – I saw him! Uncle Toyin is alive, down there in the world beneath the lake.'

'Stop it, Simi!' her mum cried angrily. 'How can you hurt me like this?'

Simi was bursting with frustration when she suddenly remembered something. She rushed into the house and came back seconds later holding the little wooden car that Toyin had given her. 'Here,' she said, handing it to her mum.

Her mum stared at it irritably until sudden recognition twisted her face. 'Where did you get this?' she whispered. 'He never let go of this stupid little thing. I spent weeks carving it for his seventh birthday.' Her voice broke and she held the little wooden car to her chest. 'I don't understand!'

Her chest heaved with a jerk and her body began to tremble so violently that Simi got scared. 'Mum!'

Iyanla moved forward swiftly and took her daughter into the house. Simi followed, relieved to leave the scrutinizing eyes of the villagers.

'Mum! I didn't mean to upset you!' Simi cried. All at once she felt the weight of the past days and the whole terrible experience hit her. She broke into tears. 'I'm so sorry, Mum!'

'Did you really see him? Please tell me the truth, Simi. Why didn't he come back?' Her mum's eyes were wide and confused and blurred with tears.

'He could not leave, my daughter.' Iyanla spoke so gently that Simi looked at her in surprise. 'Biola, remember your brother how he really was. Remember his dreamy eyes, his straying thoughts and distant look. He was a gift not intended for keeping. Just to be borrowed by us for a brief, happy moment.'

Her mum shuddered and nodded.

'He said he wanted you to think of him and be happy, Mum,' Simi added softly.

'Oh no!' her mum gasped. She was crying now as she sat in the little living room, holding her arms tightly across her chest. She began to rock herself back and forth. 'I am so sorry, Iyanla. Mama, please forgive me.'

Iyanla sat down beside her and placed a hand

on her daughter's back.

Simi knelt down in front of the sofa on which they sat and cuddled against their legs.

The sounds of drumming and singing trailed into the house. The celebrations of the relieved and happy villagers were beginning. But Simi did not want to join in just yet, she was happy to be exactly where she was. They sat like that for a long time, holding each other.

Simi smiled as a thought came to her: this is how grandmothers, mothers and daughters should be.

Author's note

Children of the Quicksands was inspired by the place of my childhood. I grew up in a little town in the south-west of Nigeria where I had an adventurous and never-boring childhood. We lived in the university staff quarters at the very edge of town and beyond our house there was nothing but bushes, farms and forests.

My siblings, friends and I would go on adventures, running through the bushes – barefoot on red earth – watching out for snakes and scorpions. With my little sister perched on my back we would scale fences and farm gates in search of mango trees, slide down a secret red valley and explore a vast stretch of dry land we called 'Desert'. Sometimes we would also sneak to the forbidden lake. It was a little lake enclosed by whispery trees and dusty bushes, with muddy red water and slippery banks that were like quicksand.

There was something absolutely magical about that place that never left me.

I loved sharing these memories with my daughters and searched for children's books that tell similar fun or adventurous experiences of Nigeria or Africa – but to my dismay, I couldn't find any. So I decided to write *Children of the Quicksands* for them so they (and hopefully other kids) could see themselves in a book and be excited about Nigerian adventures.

Nigeria is full of magic, legends, adventure, courage, beauty, love and friendship and I hope that with my story I have brought some of all that to you.

Acknowledgements

I am extremely lucky to have a very supportive and wonderful family. First thanks go to them. My mum who inspired my passion for reading through her own love of books. Thank you for being my number one reader and for your sharp and patient eye.

My dad who never seemed surprised when we came home as kids carrying any medals or prizes. Thank you for having that faith in your children and for giving us that boldness to aim high.

My sister Elele and my brothers Osebo and Odia. You are the best! I love our chat group where I can throw in any questions or voice my fears, however stupid they may seem. You are always there for me.

My husband, Boubacar, all this would not have been possible without you. Thank you for taking me and my dreams seriously.

My daughters and inspiration, Shola, Enina and Leila, thank you for those wonderful evenings when you allowed me to read my stories to you.

For your excitement about Simi, asking for more, making me finish writing *Children of the Quicksands* faster than ever.

Dayo, my self-nominated 'manager-in-law' who showed me the magic of Epe and is also my Yoruba translator.

I am also grateful to the rest of my family and friends who have been there for me, strengthening my ever-doubting spirit.

A big thank you to the judges of the 2019 *Times*/Chicken House Children's Fiction Competition, for choosing my book from among so many. Barry Cunningham, Alex O'Connell, Florentyna Martin, Nikesh Shukla, Nikki Gamble, Amy Fitzgerald, Becca Langton and Gracie Joslin.

To Barry Cunningham, for that unbelievable phone call that made me fall off the sofa. For the honour of wearing his famous hat and for everything else.

To Rachel Leyshon, my lovely editor whose suggestions often pushed me to the edge of my seat and caused sweat outbreaks. The outcome was wonderful.

To Elinor Bagenal, for our lovely talks, for

telling me my book is unique and for selling it to the world.

A huge thank you to Jazz Bartlett Love and Laura Myers and all the other wonderful people at Chicken House who have been so supportive.

Thank you to Adamma Okonkwo for her very helpful feedback, and to Daphne Tagg.

To Helen Crawford-White for the absolutely stunning cover.

I am forever indebted to the Commonwealth Writers for choosing my short story in 2018 and giving such a huge opportunity to an unknown voice like mine. That was the beginning of everything.

And finally, thank you to all the readers who are excited about diverse books featuring other cultures and types of people. There are so many wonderful stories out here. Thank you for reading mine.